THE
BLACK
PIRATE

THE GATEWAY PAPERBACKS

THE BLACK PIRATE

JAMES CAHILL

LUTTERWORTH PRESS
GUILDFORD AND LONDON

First Paperback edition 1971
Second impression 1977
Reprinted 1980

ISBN 0 7188 1827 X

Printed in Great Britain
by Fletcher & Son Ltd, Norwich

CONTENTS

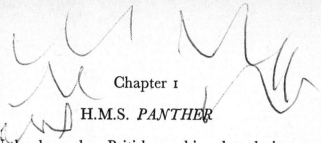

Chapter 1

H.M.S. *PANTHER*

IN the days when British warships chased pirates in Chinese waters, H.M.S. *Panther*, an ancient river gunboat, rocked gently at anchor. On her bridge paced a keen-eyed snotty, with his telescope under his arm, and up in the crows' nest the look-out was just as vigilant. In the distance, dimly outlined in the moonlight, the waves were breaking on an inhospitable shore.

The sea murmured and gurgled against the gunboat's sides; occasionally a rope slapped or some tackle creaked; but the night was very silent. Jack Hawkins, the snotty, paced up and down and wished that something would happen.

A step sounded lightly on the deck, and he glanced over the side. Yes, the Captain of the gunboat, Lieutenant Burgoyne, was coming to relieve him. He yawned, stretched, and then came smartly to the salute.

"All quiet?" queried Lieutenant Burgoyne.

"All quiet, sir. As usual! Nothing ever happens off this coast, it seems to me."

"Ah, you never know," said the Lieutenant absently, scanning the misty horizon. "O.K., Snotty. You turn in."

"Ay, ay sir." But Jack Hawkins did not go immediately. The look-out's relief was climbing the ratlines, and his gaze followed the man up. "I suppose that's necessary, sir?"

7

"What?" Lieutenant Burgoyne put down his telescope, with which he had been inspecting the shore.

"Stationing a look-out, sir. I mean, we've been here close on a week, and not even a seagull has visited us!"

"We're not here for the convenience of sea-gulls," said the Lieutenant drily. "And I'm not in the habit of stationing men in unnecessary positions, either."

"Sorry, sir!" murmured Jack.

"You want to know what it's all about, I suppose?" asked Burgoyne, focusing the glass again.

"Well, sir—it would be more fun if I knew what to look out for, if you see what I mean!"

"Fun isn't exactly what we're here for either!"

"No sir. Definitely not sir! I quite see that, sir. But then—why?"

"Ever heard of the Black Pirate?" asked Lieutenant Burgoyne.

Jack chuckled.

"I used to read about him when I was a kid, sir. Why?"

"Oh, only because we're looking for him, that's all."

Midshipman Jack Hawkins was silent, wondering if the Lieutenant was laughing at him. Lieutenant Burgoyne read his thoughts and laughed softly.

"I knew that'd be your reaction! All you fellows straight out from home think that pirates are a thing of the past, and that the China coast

is as safe as Piccadilly. That's why I've said
nothing hitherto. You wouldn't have taken it
seriously. You don't now! But it's true, all the
same."

"If you say it's true, sir—" said Jack in some
perplexity.

"I do. It is true. It's one of the tragedies of
this part of the world. The people are good,
kindly folk, but the pirates swoop down and rob
them of all they possess—of their lives too,
sometimes. It's no new thing, of course—there
have always been pirates in these waters, and
from time to time we have to take a hand in
cleaning them up. This is one of those times.
That's all."

"Then there really is a Black Pirate?" asked
Jack almost incredulously.

"There certainly is! He's not just a story in
a boy's magazine, I can assure you."

"And he's operating in this part of the world?"

"Ah, that I can't tell you with equal assurance.
In fact, our information is none too reliable, and
very scanty at that."

"But you think he is, sir?"

"I've been told that he is, and I hope he is."

"But where, sir?"

"Up that river, I suspect. That is to say, I've
worked it out that his headquarters might be up
there. If I'm right then he's either there, and
will have to come out some time, or else he's out
and will want to go home some time. In either
case we catch him."

"And if you're wrong, sir?"

"If I'm wrong, Snotty, we shall just sit here until our beards grow so long that they foul the propellors! Now cut along off to bed."

Jack swung off down the companionway and glanced, in passing, into the lower mess deck. There slung hammocks with their snoring occupants seemed to fill the dimly lighted smoky apartment, but there were still a few men sitting at the tables, bent low to avoid the hammocks just above their heads, writing letters home.

Jack tapped one burly seaman on the head.

"Give them my love, Binns."

The man looked up with a grin.

"Ay, ay, sir"

Jack chuckled. Charley Binns had been the gardener's boy before he had joined the Navy and followed Master Jack across the sea. Many was the time that they had gone off into the woods together, with a borrowed gun, after rabbits, and many were the lickings they had deserved and endured at the hands of their long-suffering parents for their wild behaviour all over the countryside. But there was no harm in either of them. A pair of high-spirited lads, they had caused some consternation in the village before the Navy provided an outlet for their superfluous energy.

Now Jack was of a mind to impart the exciting information he had just acquired to his old confederate.

"Ever seen a pirate, Binns?"

Binns had returned to his letter, but he looked up with a grin.

"On the pictures."

"Well, you're quite likely to see one in the flesh any time now, the Owner says!"

"Coo!" Binns said, much impressed.

"The Black Pirate," said Jack, leaning against the wall. "We think his headquarters are up the river and we're lying in wait for him."

"Coo!" said Binns again. He turned as a short, stocky little man with a leathery face approached. "Hear that, Mr. Hardbake?"

Petty Officer Hardbake nodded.

"Pirates!" he said expressively. "I bin fighting Chinese pirates, off an' on, ever since I were a boy, I have! Not that they're Chinese, really, not in the strict sense of the word, if you see what I mean."

"I don't, quite," said Jack Hawkins with a grin. "How can a Chinese pirate not be Chinese?"

"Well, sir, it's like this. Some of 'em's Chinese, I dare say, but the most of 'em's just sweepin's —sweepin's of all the dregs o' the Eastern ports. There's Malayans, there's Japs, there's every sort of low dog you can think of, an' they gets 'em a junk an' sails for the rivers o' China an' preys on the poor, hardworkin' folk o' the land."

"I always thought that pirates were things you read about but very rarely met," said Jack.

"That may be so, sir. They takes good care as you don't meet 'em too often. Given you're a British gunboat, when you meets 'em you hangs 'em an' that's a very good reason for not meetin' with us more'n they can help."

"I see your point," nodded Jack. "What's

up?" he added sharply, seeing the Petty Officer throw back his head in a listening attitude.

"I heard the look-out give a shout, sir."

"Did you? I heard nothing."

"Yes sir. Object on the port bow, sir. Think I'll go on deck, sir."

"I'll come with you." Midshipman Jack Hawkins went swiftly up the companionway, followed by Petty Officer Hardbake and Ordinary Seaman Binns. He found Lieutenant Burgoyne focusing his telescope into the uncertain light towards the shore.

"What is it, sir?"

"A sampan, I think. Got your binoculars with you?"

"Yes, sir." Jack slung his glasses round and stared across the heaving sea. There was something out there, but he was not prepared to say exactly what it was just yet.

"It's a sampan, sir," said Petty Officer Hardbake, screwing up his bright blue eyes.

"You've got eyes like a hawk, Hardbake!"

"Not so bad, sir, though I says it myself. Yes, it's a sampan, an' there's a coolie in it."

"Well, we'll wait and see what he wants. A single solitary coolie doesn't seem much of a menace." The Captain glanced up at the look-out and hailed him softly. "We'll keep our eyes on this chap. You keep yours skinned on the rest of the horizon—I don't want anyone to creep up on us while we're watching this bird."

"Ay, ay sir."

Jack was tingling with excitement. This was

the first strange thing to happen to him since he had come out from home to join his ship. Not that in itself the arrival of a coolie in a sampan was strange, but at that time of night and after all he had been hearing about pirates he was sure that there must be something strange in the adventure. Perhaps the newcomer would have something to tell them about the Black Pirate.

This last thought had also occurred to both Lieutenant Burgoyne and Petty Officer Hardbake. There was no other reason, as far as they could see, why the man should be rowing out to the gunboat, unless, of course, it was a blind and there was to be an attack from another quarter while he parleyed with them.

Slowly, so slowly, the sampan came nearer, until they could hear the splash of the long oar. At last the coolie was near enough for them to see him plainly, and Lieutenant Burgoyne hailed him. Jack was keenly disappointed that the conversation that followed was in a tongue that he could not understand.

"He's coming aboard," said Burgoyne, turning to the Petty Officer.

"I got that too, sir."

"Pity you don't understand the lingo, Hawkins," said Burgoyne.

"Yes sir," said Jack, agreeing heartily.

The sampan ran alongside and its occupant tied it up and then swarmed up, disdaining the hand held out to him by the Petty Officer. Jack looked at the man, naked except for billowing but ragged trousers, as he faced them on the deck, and thought with admiration what a fine specimen he was.

During the talk that followed Jack had only the muttered information of Petty Officer Hardbake to guide him, but it was enough. The Lieutenant and the Chinese talked earnestly for some time, and Hardbake listened and translated in brief snatches. Jack listened eagerly.

"Yes—he's from the river," muttered Hardbake. "Yes, he's got news of the Black Pirate. H'm! Yes, wants to lead a party to attack him. H'm. H'm. Says his farm's bin burned an' all his cattle carried off. Says they've killed his old mother an' father—dear, dear! Yes, now he's sayin' what he wants the Lieutenant to do to the Black Pirate when he catches 'im, but I doubt that plan'll meet with approval! No, not our way. Poor lad, though. You kin understand 'im feelin' that way."

Jack wished that he could understand what the man was saying for himself, since the Petty Officer did not translate just what the young man wanted to do to the Black Pirate, but he could see from the expression on Burgoyne's face that it was something pretty horrible. Finally the Captain spoke.

"Petty Officer, take this man and give him some food," he said. "And then come back to me on the bridge. Will you come with me now, Mr. Hawkins? There's something I want to talk over with you."

Chapter 2

AN EXPEDITION

LIEUTENANT Burgoyne walked up and down the bridge of H.M.S. *Panther*, deep in thought, while his second-in-command, Midshipman Jack Hawkins, watched him curiously.

"The facts are these," said Burgoyne abruptly. "That coolie brought news that the Black Pirate is camped up the river—just as I thought, in fact —and that he is conducting a series of raids over the countryside. He wants me to attack him at once to prevent further bloodshed. The scoundrel is killing and plundering for miles around, and probably may not come down the river for months—until this part of the country is drained dry."

"Well, can't we attack now, sir?" asked Jack eagerly. "What's to stop us?"

"He's built a boom," said Burgoyne slowly. "Apparently he's on the look-out for attack. He's dug himself in for as long as he wants to stay there—cunning brute! As soon as he's done all he wants to do in these parts he'll lift the boom and sail his rotten old junk downstream, but meanwhile it's a pretty efficient piece of work, and according to the coolie I don't think we could tackle it."

"Couldn't we blow it out of the water, sir?"

"I've half a mind to try another way first."

"What's that, sir?"

"Go overland and take him in the rear."

"Oh!" Jack Hawkins was surprised, and began to turn the idea over in his mind.

"It's what we have to do often enough in these waters, turn ourselves into soldiers," said Burgoyne with a slight smile.

Petty Officer Hardbake stepped on to the bridge, and saluted.

"I've fed 'im, sir, an' now 'e's restin'," he said.

"Good. What do you make of him, Hardbake?"

"I think he's trustworthy, sir."

"You had a talk to him, I suppose?"

"I did, sir, an' he struck me as being the goods. He's no spy, sir."

"Did you think he was a spy, sir?" ejaculated Jack.

"There's always that possibility, you know," said Burgoyne drily. "He might have been sent to lead us into an ambush. What did he tell you about the river, Hardbake?"

"Just the same as 'e told you, sir. The boom, an' that. I think 'e's on the level, sir."

"Actually, so do I, but I wanted to have your opinion. Well! I suppose we've got to take advantage of this information, eh?"

"I reckon so, sir. Not often we gets a Black Pirate handed to us on a silver tray, so to speak, eh?"

"You're quite right. Now the position is this. You and I have sailed together for a good many years, Hardbake, and I trust your judgment."

"Thank you, sir," said the Petty Officer quietly.

"Now, either you and Mr. Hawkins go and

cope with this scoundrel, or I go, leaving you and Mr. Hawkins in charge of the ship."

"Couldn't do that, sir," said the Petty Officer, shaking his head.

"Couldn't do what?"

"Well, beggin' 'is pardon, you couldn't go orf leavin' a young gentleman of Mr. Hawkins's experience in charge of the ship."

"You've got all the experience needed, Hardbake, and Mr. Hawkins knows that he can rely on you. And, besides that, I have every confidence in Mr. Hawkins himself."

"Thank you, sir. And I'm sure that, with Petty Officer Hardbake behind me, I could manage all right. But—don't you feel, sir, that it's a job for a younger man?"

"I'm not exactly senile, Hawkins," said the Lieutenant drily. He was still on the sunny side of thirty.

"Oh, I know, sir. But—"

"It won't do, sir," said Petty Officer Hardbake, shaking his head.

"You mean you want a crack at him yourself?"

"'Tain't that, sir. Leastways, 'tain't only that. I do admit as I've a sort o' longin' to git to grips with 'im, after what that coolie said, but it's this, sir, too. Supposin'—what ain't likely, o' course—but supposin' as the expedition don't come back. It puts Mr. 'Awkins in a difficult position."

"Midshipmen have been in as difficult a position before, Hardbake, and have done well."

"Yes sir, but 'e's got to decide whether to come

on in an' try to rescue what's left o' you, sir, or whether to run for 'elp, in a manner o' speakin'. An' whichever way he goes he's liable to regret it all 'is life. If 'e takes a chance an' comes in, an' gits cut orf an' cut up, he'll regret the waste of lives. An' if he sends for reinforcements an' waits for 'em, an' then finds 'e could've saved you alive if he'd come in sooner, then 'e'll regret that too, all 'is days. I submit, sir, as the decision is too 'ard for a young man without experience to carry on 'is shoulders. I submit, sir, that him an' me ought to take the expedition ashore, an' you, sir, stop be'ind."

"I don't like your conclusions, Hardbake, but your reasoning is sound," sighed Lieutenant Burgoyne. "Very well. Is that your opinion, too, Mr. Hawkins?"

"Well sir, I like the Petty Officer's conclusions but not his reasoning, sir. But it seems to come to the same thing. I'd like to take the expedition sir."

"Yes, I know you would! Very well. I can spare you a dozen men. Is there anyone particular you'd like to take?"

"I'd like to take Binns, sir."

"Ordinary Seaman Binns. What about you, Hardbake?"

"Leading Seaman Stacey, sir. Ship's marksman, sir."

"An excellent choice."

"And the Bren gun party, sir."

"And a couple of machine-guns, I suppose. Very good."

"I suppose the coolie is prepared to act as guide, sir?" asked Jack.

"Oh yes, that's all fixed up. Now, will you take over here for a moment or two, Mr. Hardbake? I want to have a word with Mr. Hawkins in my cabin."

"Ay, ay, sir," said the Petty Officer, and the two officers went below.

"Sit down, Jack," said Burgoyne as soon as they got into his cabin.

Jack did so, looking and feeling rather surprised, for there was a note of almost affectionate anxiety in the voice of the man whom he had hitherto known only as a brisk, business-like captain.

"Now look here," continued Burgoyne, speaking almost as an elder brother might have done, "I want to give you a few hints. To begin with, my reluctance to let you go on this expedition does not arise from any distrust of your courage or powers of initiative—I hope you understand that?"

"Thank you, sir," said Jack.

"But it does arise from misgivings about your inexperience in these waters. It's no joke, my lad, to go against a crafty, fully armed pirate, who knows the country as he knows the palm of his hand and who is as ruthless and cruel as he is tough. Your being British won't help you, you know, if he gets hold of you. In fact, it might inflame him to greater cruelties! Don't suppose that he has any fear of us in his black heart! And you'll be outnumbered. But the superiority

in weapons lies with you. Now my advice is this
—don't let yourself be surprised and ambushed.
Send out scouts before you move a yard. And
post sentries at every stop. Remember that
you're in a hostile country. And take the advice
of Hardbake, even when it conflicts with your
own opinion. He knows the country, and you
can be sure his courage is unquestionable. We've
been together in many a tight corner, old
Hardbake and I, and I can assure you that he
has the heart of a lion."

"I'm sure he has, sir," said Jack heartily. "I
can see he's a grand chap, and the lads look on
him as a father."

"Yes, they'd follow him down a shark's gullet,
I verily believe," said Burgoyne with a smile. "I
wish I were going with you!"

"It's a grand chance for me, sir!"

"It is. I hope you make the most of it. Now go
and get some rest. You'll start an hour before
dawn."

Jack went to his cabin, but before he lay down
to rest he looked over his weapons. He oiled his
revolver and made sure that his pouch was full
of ammunition. Then he tested the blade of his
dirk. Then, with a sigh, he took off his boots
and monkey jacket and lay down with his hands
behind his head, sure that he would never sleep.
But, as he was planning what he would say—
through an interpreter, unfortunately—as soon
as he had caught the Black Pirate, his eyes closed
and he was asleep.

Meanwhile Lieutenant Burgoyne had relieved

Petty Officer Hardbake on the bridge, and the latter had gone below to pick his men and to get the stores and ammunition ready. There would be little sleep that night for Petty Officer Hardbake! He prowled in the tiny gunboat's armoury and picked the Bren guns and machine-guns for his party. To an onlooker the weapons might all have looked alike, but to Hardbake each had a personality, and he chose some and put others aside until he had what he wanted.

Then the ammunition; so many cases of this, so many cases of that. And then stores, for it was estimated that the expedition might be ashore a week, and a man must be fed properly if he is to march and fight properly, thought Petty Officer Hardbake. Here, although he was no dietician and could not have discoursed on vitamins and calories, he nevertheless picked the tins that, in his opinion, would give his men what he called "guts". And it is possible that an experienced dietician would not altogether have disagreed with his choice.

Shortly before dawn Jack awoke to the touch of a hand on his shoulder, and Cooky's voice in his ear.

"Chocolate, sir. Nice hot cup o' chocolate, sir. You drink that up, an' your breakfast'll be ready in no time."

"What time is it?" murmured Jack, turning over and burying his face in the pillow.

"Now sir, that won't do, that won't! It's time to git up, that's what it is. The lads are havin' their breakfast a'ready. Come on, sir! It's a nasty cold mornin', with a nip in the air an' a wet mist all over everythink. Just the mornin' to go a-huntin' for pirates!"

"Pirates!" Jack flung himself off his bunk. "Gosh, Cooky—I'd clean forgotten! All right— I'll be along in a tick. I shan't want much breakfast, though. This cup of chocolate'll do me fine."

"You want to eat while you got the chance, sir," said Cooky, shaking a mournful head. "Who knows where you'll be to-morrow night, eh sir?"

"Get out, you old scoundrel!" laughed Jack. "All right, I'll have bacon and eggs and kidneys and kippers."

"That's a fact you won't!" grinned Cooky as he trotted off.

"And porridge," shouted Jack.

"Ay, ay, sir."

Jack was dressing hurriedly when Petty Officer Hardbake poked his head in.

"No hurry, sir. Plenty o' time. I told the lads to set down an' write a line to their mothers. There'll be no mails where we're a-goin', and we don't know when the chance'll come again."

"I'd better do that, too," said Jack, ashamed that the thought had not occurred to him.

"Very good, sir. Plenty o' time, as I said." Hardbake withdrew, and Jack scribbled a hasty line to his parents, telling them that he was going on an expedition, the importance of which could scarcely be magnified! Then he found, to his surprise, that he was very hungry after all, and went in search of food.

It was still dark—much darker, in fact, than when the coolie had come aboard—when the men stood ready on the deck for disembarkation. There was no moon, and Lieutenant Burgoyne inspected them by the light of his torch. Then, satisfied, he wished them God-speed, and they clambered down the side and dropped into the motor-boat that was to take them as far as possible up river before they took to the land. For a little while Burgoyne listened to the chug-chug of the motor-boat, and then the sound vanished in the distance. Burgoyne sighed.

"I wish I could have gone with them," he muttered to himself. "Ah well!" He resumed his lonely pacing up and down the gunboat's bridge.

Chapter 3

COLIN AT HOME

ON a little hill overlooking a small village, two figures sat under a cherry tree, gazing down at the scene of peaceful activity below them. The elder was a big man with a square black beard, and the younger was a youth of about seventeen, his son.

Few people, looking at the big man in his patched and faded khaki shirt, open at the neck, would have taken him for a minister of the Gospel, but Mr. Wedderburn belonged to the sort of clergyman who had to build his own church with his own hands, and his own house too. And not only that—periodically he would harness his old pony, pack a tent with sundry other belongings, and disappear on a tour of some hundreds of miles, preaching, marrying, burying and, most important of all—baptizing.

It was a strenuous life, but then Mr. Wedderburn was a strenuous sort of man, and the life suited him perfectly. His parishioners in that little Chinese village had viewed him with courteous suspicion at first, and presently with affectionate pity. They simply could not understand how a man could act as he did, and his enthusiasm struck them as very funny. For a long time he held his services by himself, but he had not expected quick results, and in due time, slowly, the people, having learned to trust him, began to listen to him.

He was, of course, a doctor as well as a clergy-man, and through the care of their bodies he found the way to their souls. But probably it was when he took a holiday, after five years of patient work, that they realized suddenly how much they missed him, how much they had learned to depend on him, and when he returned, bringing his bride with him, he found them much more ready to listen to his doctrine.

For one blissfully happy year, the young couple worked among their Chinese friends, but only a few weeks after their baby boy was born, Mrs. Wedderburn caught a fever from a poor woman who had wandered into the village and whom she was nursing, and died.

"Of course you will send little Colin back to England," said a visiting missionary to poor Mr. Wedderburn. "I'll take him as far as the coast with me—my wife would love to look after the little chap. She loves babies! And he's such a good little fellow—there'll be plenty of people willing to take him home for you."

"It's kind of you," said Mr. Wedderburn, "but I don't think I could bear to let him go! And besides that, the village has adopted him. I think my people here would be hurt if I took him away from their care now."

It was true. The whole village had rallied round their beloved friend and teacher, and it was clear that there would be no lack of love for little Colin. And so he grew up, playing in the dust with fat little Chinese babies, learning the arts of the Chinese schoolboy, until at last Mr.

Wedderburn knew that he must part with him for a time, so that he could go to school in England and be trained for a future career.

Colin himself did not understand why he should go.

"But Dad," he protested, "you can teach me all I want to know. Why, I'm getting on fine with arithmetic—you said so yourself!"

"I know, son," said Mr Wedderburn gently, "but there are things I can't teach you And if you want to come here and follow on after me— that is what you want to do, isn't it? I've always taken it for granted that it was "

"Of course it is, Dad. And that's what I mean. I can speak the language awfully well—Ngan Keng said so only yesterday. She said I spoke it better than I do English. She really did! And I'm sure I could take the service if you'd let me. Will you let me try, Dad? Just once?"

"I can't do that, son," smiled his father. "And though you may not think it—it's as important to be able to speak your native language correctly as it is to speak Chinese. You'll see what I mean some day. But in the meantime I'm afraid you'll have to go home to school. And then, if you work hard, to college and hospital. Then, when you're trained, you can come out here to me."

"It'll be an awful long time," said the boy wistfully.

"I'm afraid it will," said his father with a heavy sigh.

And now the first part of that "awful long

time" was over, and Colin had come out for a holiday with his father before going on to college.

"What's it feel like?" asked Mr. Wedderburn lightly, but watching his son rather anxiously all the same.

"Coming home," said Colin with a quick smile.

"Sure? You don't feel strange—like a fish out of water, eh?"

"Rather not! Did you think I should?"

"I thought you might. But I'm glad you don't. How did you like England?"

"I loved it," said Colin instantly. "I liked the old school tremendously, too. In fact, when we broke up for the last time—the last time as far as I was concerned, I mean—I felt pretty low about it."

"Well, you did pretty well," commented his father. "I was quite satisfied with your reports —on the whole."

"On the whole!" Colin grinned. "Well, I know I shall have to work now if I'm to get through the rest of my course."

"You understand now why you had to go to England? I'm afraid you thought me the worst of fathers at first for sending you away!"

"Oh, I understand now, of course. And even then I knew that there must be some very good reason if you did it, although I couldn't understand it at the time."

"You trusted me that far?"

"All the way, Dad, and all the time!" said Colin with a serene smile. "And—this isn't very easy to say, particularly when we've only just met after all these years, but I think it's time to say it—well, knowing and trusting you has made it easy to trust God. If my Heavenly Father is anything like my earthly father—"

"My boy—my boy! Don't compare me with the King of Heaven!" cried Mr. Wedderburn with emotion.

"No, I'm not making any mistake there. I know that God is King and Lord, Creator and Maker, and that it's a privilege to kneel and worship Him. It was your life that first made God real and your love that made God's love real to me. I've now come to know a lot more of what God's love is in that He sent Jesus to die for me. He is now my Saviour and I want to follow Him. But I also know that Jesus taught us to call Him Father, and since that name belongs to the most beloved and trusted person on earth, it has brought me nearer to Him by the way that our Lord evidently meant us to go."

"Well, that's that," said Colin with forced lightness. "I don't find it frightfully easy to talk about that sort of thing, you know, but somehow I wanted to say it. I couldn't follow in your footsteps or take up missionary work at all unless I really knew God myself—and that's the most important thing in the world for me—and it's due to you that I find it so. But I—I don't find it very easy to talk about."

"Neither do I, even after a lifetime of doing it," said Mr. Wedderburn thoughtfully. "Once I'm preaching, of course, I forget about myself and it comes naturally enough. Or when talking to a poor soul in trouble—"

"Or reproving an evildoer," chuckled his son.

"Well!" Mr. Wedderburn laughed. "I hope you're not going to accuse me of harshness towards yourself?"

"Towards me? No! But I do remember one or two occasions in the dim and distant past when you seemed to flame up and become very terrible. I always thought you looked like Moses before he threw the tables of the Law at the Children of Israel."

"We are not told that he threw them *at* the Children of Israel," said Mr. Wedderburn. "And I'm sure he didn't look at all like me."

"All beard and flashing eyes," grinned Colin. "I never knew what it was all about."

"Cruelty, usually. If anything roused me— and rouses me now—it's cruelty. You can't remember any of these—er—explosions in any detail, I suppose?"

"One was connected with a poor, miserable sort of chap that Ngan Keng's husband and some others brought in tied to a bamboo pole. You led off about that, I remember."

"Oh yes—he was a pirate."

"Was he, now?"

"Yes. A nasty piece of work, I'm afraid, and they knew it. Not one of the big pirate leaders, of course, but a miserable hanger-on, a throat-slitter and thief. They wanted to torture him a little and then finish him, and I had to dissuade them."

"Dissuade is a mild word!"

"Well—it had to be done."

"What happened to him?"

"To Li-Foo? He's one of my lay readers now."

"I say! Is he really?"

"Yes, and a very good man. It took time, of course—time and patience, but he's a changed man now."

"I shouldn't have thought it possible!"

"Ah, perhaps it is in this sort of work more than in any other that we learn the truth of our Lord's saying that with man it is impossible, but with God all things are possible."

"I suppose so." Colin sat in thought for a minute or two. "It must be rather marvellous to see things like that happening under your very eyes," he said wistfully. "Men changed, and all that. I hope it happens to me some day."

"I hope it does, son. But remember—patience! It doesn't happen in five minutes, and if it does— distrust it. No, I don't mean that, exactly, but don't expect a lightning conversion to bring forth fruits of the Spirit all at once. The conversion may be perfectly sound, but you may get sore disappointments before the convert's feet are well and truly set on the way. A man may profess great and wonderful things, and you can tell by the light on his face that he is sincere, and yet to-morrow or the day after he may do a dirty trick that belongs to the old life. Don't be disappointed. Gently—like as a father pitieth his children, you know—gently lead him on, and in time, with patience— Well, here am I lecturing you as though you were ready for the mission field immediately! Come along—it's time for evensong."

And as he spoke the bell of the little church down in the village began to peal, and out of the huts and cottages the villagers began to stroll towards their church.

Chapter 4

BANDITS

THE days passed very pleasantly in the little
village. Colin went about with his father a good
deal, but he also renewed acquaintance with the
friends of his childhood. At first some of them
were a little shy, but they soon found that he had
not really changed, and then they talked and
joked with him as freely as in the good old days.

How he loved it all! He was gently scolded
by plump, kindly Ngan Keng, the woman who
had practically adopted him when his mother
had died, and had brought him up with her own
considerable brood. Now she told him that he was
as bad as ever—tearing his clothes scrambling over
the hills and making them muddy in the streams.
He laughed and put his arm round her shoulders.

"Will you whip me for a naughty boy?"

"I never whipped you!" She looked reproach-
fully at him out of her big, kind, brown eyes.

"Ah, you were always far too gentle with us all.
Why didn't you whip us, Little Mother? We
were very naughty, Soo-Chu and I."

Now Soo-Chu was her favourite son, and she
smiled at this outrageous remark.

"I never whip little boys. When they do
wrong I tell them so, and then they do not do it
another time."

Colin laughed and hugged her. The Chinese
are very kind to little children, and he could
remember many a time in his early days when a

good whipping had been deserved but never administered.

"You were too good to us," he said.

"Poor little motherless one," she said softly.

"You were my mother," said Colin affectionately, and indeed his own mother could not have looked after him more devotedly.

"And now you go fishing?" she asked, changing the subject, for praise always made her feel shy.

"Yes, to-morrow at dawn."

"For a week, Soo-Chu tells me."

"Yes, a real expedition. It'll take us three days to reach the big river, and then the place he wants to take me to is two *li* beyond that. In fact, I shall be surprised if we are back in a week, Ngan Keng. We shall stay as long as the fish are biting."

"Well, the village could do with some fish," she said, nodding approbation. "Bring back all you can."

"We shall eat all we can, and bring back the rest," grinned Colin.

"Yes, yes! You are greedy boys," she said. "Now I must pack food for your journey. Do you eat only English food now that you have been so long away from us, or will you eat the same as Soo-Chu?"

"The same as Soo-Chu, of course," exclaimed Colin. "And plenty of it."

The two boys set off at dawn the following day, laden with gear, but full of buoyant anticipation. Mr. Wedderburn saw them go without an anxious thought. He little knew that one of them he was never to see again!

After the first few miles Colin wondered how ever he was going to keep pace with Soo-Chu's tireless coolie lope, but presently it all came back to him, and his fatigue fell from him like a discarded cloak. The comfortable jog-trot that had once been second nature to him became easy once more, and Soo-Chu grinned as he saw his companion's returned ease of progress.

"Now you are no more an Englishman," he said with great satisfaction. "Before you talk like a Chinese, you dress like a Chinese, but you walk like a foreign devil. Now you look altogether Chinese."

"Splendid," said Colin. "I haven't forgotten the language much, have I?"

"Not at all. In some words there is a wrong accent, but not many. By the time this trip is over, you will talk quite properly again."

"There is one thing that's wrong, I know," said Colin. "When I went away I was a child and spoke like a child, and much was forgiven me because I was only a child. But now I must learn to speak to my elders without giving offence. It would be terrible if I talked to some old mandarin with the freedom of childhood—at my age!"

The thought amused Soo-Chu so much that he had to sit down and laugh in comfort. To a Chinese it was funny, of course. Politeness is with them is a very important thing, and although everything is overlooked in a child, in a young man like Colin any lapse in courtesy would be a very dreadful thing indeed. There is elaborate eti-

34

quette and ceremonial to cover all the everyday dealings of life—a Chinese does not simply walk into a shop and buy what he wants as we do; there is much polite conversation to be gone through first. And so if a strapping young man like Colin started talking to a well-bred Chinese with the freedom of a child, it would be a much more astonishing and dreadful thing than if such a thing happened in England.

Soo-Chu, when he had recovered from his mirth, took quite as serious a view of the matter as Colin, and they decided that for the duration of their trip—or for some days, at least—they would conduct themselves as two elderly mandarins, talking ceremoniously about their journey, their meals, their sleeping arrangements; and any casual encounter on their way should be treated in the same way. They carried out this plan fairly well, with occasionally breakdowns when Colin forgot, and thus reduced Soo-Chu to helpless laughter. The young Chinese lad had an easily tickled sense of humour, and would roll on the ground, shedding his burdens in all directions, when some unguarded remark of Colin's amused him. Then Colin would pick up the rolled-up mat, the parcel of food and the fishing tackle dropped by his friend and sit patiently on a rock until he was ready to continue.

"There flows the river," said Soo-Chu, waving his hands towards the horizon, and following up his remark with a long quotation about rivers from one of the old poets.

This Colin was able to cap, for Ngan Keng's

husband was a scholarly man, and in the evenings, after a day working in the fields, would sometimes read aloud from the ancient literature of his people. Colin remembered scraps and odds and ends that had caught his childish fancy in those far-off days, and now with great pride brought out a quotation that matched Soo-Chu's.

"That was good," said the Chinese lad approvingly.

"I remembered it," said Colin. "Your father often quoted it—it was one of his favourites, wasn't it?"

"Oh yes."

"Does he still read aloud to you all in the evenings?"

"His eyes are not as good as they were, and sometimes he tells me to read for him. Or one of my brothers. But since most of them have now married and left home, usually I do the reading for him."

"And he still reads the same things?"

"Not quite. Your father got him a Bible in the Chinese tongue, and mostly we read from that now. Not always, for your father said there was much of value and beauty in our ancient writings, and that pleased my father very much. He was ready to cast them out if your father had said he must do so, but he was glad that he might still read in them sometimes."

"Ha-ha! You've forgotten now!" Colin said with a triumphant grin. "You should have said 'Your esteemed father, whose knowledge and wisdom is as the shade of a mighty oak tree in a rocky country, where the traveller may find rest and refreshment—!' Isn't that right?"

"Something like that," admitted Soo-Chu.

"Well, well! To think that I should have to give you lessons in courtesy!" Colin grinned.

Soo-Chu made a gesture of mock threatening, and Colin began to run through the reeds that led to the river bank. Suddenly, as he ran, a fusillade of shots rang out and he felt a sharp stinging pain in his shoulder, which spun him round like a top and flung him to the ground.

For a moment he lay there, wondering what on earth could have happened. Shots! The blow on his shoulder! He put up his hand to the place and it came away warm and sticky with blood. So he had been shot! His mind began to work again, and he nearly shouted for Soo-Chu. Then he realized that it would be dangerous to do so, and rolled over to try to see what had happened to his friend.

He saw him. Soo-Chu was lying face downwards among the reeds, some little distance away, and two ugly-looking men were bending over him. They raised themselves and one kicked the motionless form contemptuously. Then he saw Colin, and both raced towards him.

Colin got to his feet and awaited them. Quite useless to try to run away or hide, he knew. As well as their guns, the men carried long knives, and these were plucked from their belts and held ready as they reached him.

Alas for the recent tuition in correct Chinese! After the first rapid exchange of speech one of the

37

men seized Colin by the front of his blouse and pulled him nearer.

"Where do you come from, then?" he growled.

"Over there," said Colin vaguely, waving an arm towards the sea.

"Over where? You speak with a strange accent my lad! Now then—out with it! Who and what are you?"

"He's a foreign devil," exclaimed the second man. "Look at his skin!" He tore Colin's blouse and pointed to his chest. "Look!"

"Ah!" The first man put away his knife. "A good thing I did not slit his throat at once, eh? If there are white men about, that is a matter for the Black Pirate, eh? Tie him up and bring him along for questioning."

"My shoulder is bleeding," said Colin, as the second man brought a length of rope from some concealed pocket in his rags.

"What is that to us?"

"Well, I shall not be much use for questioning if I die on the road," said Colin.

"That is true," said the second man. He produced some grimy rags. "I will tie it up."

"I can manage," said Colin hastily, and brought out a moderately clean handkerchief, with which he somewhat awkwardly padded the wound. The other man roughly and impatiently tied the pad in place, and then Colin's hands were tied behind him and a rope halter put around his neck.

"Now, march," said the bandit.

"What about my companion?" asked Colin, trying to see if Soo-Chu had moved.

38

"Dead," said the man callously. "He was not a foreign devil, eh?"

"No, but he was my friend," said Colin.

"He has gone to his ancestors now," said the bandit, and jerked the halter.

"Will you let me bury him?" asked Colin.

"That carrion? Throw him in the river."

"No, he was my friend. Let me bury him."

The villainous men looked at him with perplexity.

"It would be less trouble to slit your throat," said the first one. He took his knife from is belt suggestively.

"The Black Pirate, your master, would not be pleased at that, though," said Colin.

"What do you know of the Black Pirate?" asked the man uneasily.

Colin tried to laugh unconcernedly.

"Wait and see! But first let me bury my friend."

"It can do no harm," said the second man.

"Go then," said the other, casting loose the halter. The two men sat down with their rifles across their knees, watching.

Colin went over to where Soo-Chu was lying and bent down beside him. It was too true—his friend was dead. With anger in his heart, he found a flat stone, and with his uninjured arm began to scrape a shallow grave in the loose, sandy soil.

It took time, but at last the task was done, and he knelt to say a prayer over the grave. Then he rejoined his captors.

"I am ready," he said. "Now take me to the Black Pirate."

Chapter 5

THE BLACK PIRATE

IT was nightfall when they reached the camp of the Black Pirate. Colin was nearly exhausted, and the pain of his wounded shoulder was considerable. His captors had not spared him, but had hurried along as if regretting the time spent on the burial of Soo-Chu, and Colin knew that a plea for a rest would have met with a brusque refusal, and therefore kept his mouth shut.

They had crossed the river in a leaky sampan and had passed a junk, well hidden from view from the main stream in a tiny, reed-filled creek. The junk had a weather-worn, deserted appearance until their sampan passed it, and then a shock-headed individual armed with a rifle had poked his head out of a port-hole and shouted some words in an almost unintelligible dialect.

Colin was able to understand his captor's reply, to the effect that he was a foreign devil prisoner.

"Let me poke his eyes out," suggested the amiable sentry, but the guards were of the opinion that their master would prefer the prisoner all in one piece until he had questioned him.

"Keep him until I come, then," said the sentry. "We'll have some fun! I'm tired of standing here, seeing no one all day. I could do with a bit of sport when my turn of duty here is over."

Colin paid no heed outwardly to this conversation, but it must be admitted that it aroused very unpleasant feelings inside. It looked as though the Black Pirate were one of the real old type of bandit, with no regard for human life or suffering, and the thought crept unbidden into Colin's mind that perhaps he had seen his father and the pleasant little village for the last time.

For a second, as this thought occurred to him, panic invaded his soul, but he crushed it down. He bowed his head for a moment and sent up a swift prayer for strength, and by the time that his captors had run the sampan into the bank and jerked his halter as a sign that he was to get out, he was in command of himself again.

Now the two bandits began to talk in low voices among themselves, and from the little that he was able to overhear, Colin realized that his continued equanimity was beginning to worry them. They expected an attempt to escape, perhaps, although it was quite clear that no such attempt could succeed. Or they expected pleas for mercy, offerings of rewards if they would set their prisoner free. But Colin knew these sort of men too well by repute to suppose that anything he could say or do would persuade them to release him. It was his calmness in his terrible situation that puzzled them completely.

After they left the sampan their way was over much more difficult country, rising at last into steep, rocky hills. Colin was feeling faint and dizzy by now, and the jerks on his halter were frequent. He stumbled, and, not having the use of his hands, could not save himself when he fell. This amused his guards, who jerked the halter purposely to make him fall, and then laughed uproariously when he did so.

Gritting his teeth, Colin kept on. What he was to do or say when he met the Black Pirate he did not know, but in his mind ran dimly the advice given to St. Paul, not to think in advance what to say when brought up before unbelievers, but to trust in God and the words would be given him. He hung to that, and hoped that he, too, would be told what to say in answer to the Black Pirate's questioning.

One thing bothered him, though he tried to put it out of his mind, and that was the fear that the Black Pirate might somehow learn of the contented little village where Mr. Wedderburn ministered to his flock, and descend upon it with his marauding band without warning and wipe it out. He was sure—or hopeful, at any rate— that so far the Black Pirate had not heard of the village. He was a good four days' journey from it, and might embark on his junk and sail away to other parts without troubling them unless he were told of their existence. But Colin was afraid that under questioning he might betray his father and friends. He knew that Chinese pirates were experts in the use of torture to their victims.

He was stumbling along in the dim twilight when he heard a hoarse shout ahead of them. One of the guards answered, and he heard the click of a rifle bolt nearby. Then they went on again, and he was aware of a shadowy form that loomed up for a moment beside them and was left behind again. They had passed the first of the Black Pirate's sentries.

Over rocks, through brush and scrub, tripping over boulders, slipping on steep ascents, so at last the trio came to their destination. Rounding a huge rock that jutted out of the side of the hill, with a sheer drop on the other side, they came to a small plateau on which a smoky fire was burning.

Colin felt the tension on his halter relax, and fell to the ground, semi-conscious. Dimly he heard fierce voices, but he could not move. Then his halter was jerked and he tried to get up but was too weak to do so. Rough hands seized him and dragged him into the circle of firelight, throwing him to the ground at the feet of a man who was evidently the Black Pirate himself.

Colin lay still, trying to master his swimming senses. He heard question and answer going on above him, and then one of the men tore his blouse open still more to show his white skin. Then he heard a cruel laugh, and words which penetrated his consciousness like a knife.

"White, eh? English or American, I suppose. Well, where there is one there will be others. We will persuade this young man to tell us how to reach his friends before we kill him. There is sure to be booty where there are English or Americans."

Colin heard the roar of savage laughter that greeted this remark, and then lost consciousness altogether. The Black Pirate—a man who had earned his title by his swarthy complexion, showing a mixture of Malay and Negro blood— bent down again and regarded him indifferently.

"Put him aside while we eat," he said. "If he wakes, give him water. And remember, no sport until we have spoken! I want to know who his friends are and where they are, too. Perhaps they are wealthy and would pay a ransom. Perhaps they are near, and can be ambushed with ease. When I have done with him you shall have him."

Colin was seized and tossed aside like a sack, and the pirates went on with their preparations for a meal. Presently he came to, and moved stiffly, with a stifled groan.

"Our little pigeon wakes up," shouted the Black Pirate seizing a brand from the flaming fire. He went over to where Colin was lying and held it so that the light fell on his captive's face. "You are awake, eh?"

"Yes, but very stiff and thirsty," said Colin, trying to keep all apprehension out of his voice and manner. But the swarthy face bent down near to his own was very terrifying, with its cruel mouth, its glittering eyes, and its lank, black locks falling in profusion down to the shoulders. Gold earrings glistened among the tangled hair, and a woman's bangle set with diamonds shone on the wrist that held the torch. Colin stared at the man, and determined whatever came not to show fear.

"Thirsty, eh, my bantam cock?" grinned the man. He shouted an order over his shoulder. "And stiff too! What a pity. Get to your feet!"

Colin rose clumsily.

44

"Will you untie my hands, please?" he said firmly.

The Black Pirate laughed.

"No, no, my little bantam! You might show fight, and I should be afraid of you!"

A roar of fierce laughter greeted this witticism, and a man walked up with a skinful of some liquid, which he held to Colin's mouth. The lad drank, though it was unpleasant and fiery, but his mouth and throat were so dry that he could not refuse.

"Now that my lord is refreshed," said the Black Pirate ironically, "perhaps he will deign to walk a little nearer the fire and answer a few trifling questions?"

"Certainly," said Colin, and accompanied his captor to a place near the fire, where the Black Pirate gave him permission to sit, by the simple expedient of nudging him so violently with his shoulder that he fell down. Then the man sat down on a heap of saddles, and the pirates closed up nearer to hear what was going on.

"Tell me, my lord," said the Black Pirate with tremendous politeness, "where were you going when my men persuaded you to visit me?"

"I was going on a fishing expedition," said Colin.

"Indeed."

"That much is true. They carried rods and reels," said one of the captors.

"Well, you were going fishing. With a solitary coolie?"

"Yes."

45

"Why?"

"I do not understand. To catch fish, of course."

"Where had you come from?"

"England."

"Eh?" The Pirate blinked.

"From England."

"You came from England to go fishing on this miserable little river? What sort of fools' talk is this? Tell me where you came from, or I shall have to persuade you!"

"You do not believe because you do not understand," said Colin boldly. "In my country a life of adventure is considered a good thing for a youth. It hardens him, and fits him for his proper work in the world."

"That I can understand," said the Black Pirate doubtfully. "What is this work for which you are fitting yourself by fishing in the inconsiderable rivers of China?"

Colin drew a deep breath, and realized that his chances for effective witness had come.

"My work is to teach the people of this land about the one true God," he said steadily. "If you will listen to me I will tell you of the Saviour Who alone can save you from your sins, in this life and the next."

"Me?" cried the pirate. "But this is missionary talk. I have heard missionaries. Is it for this that you are here?"

"Yes," said Colin.

The man looked at him doubtfully.

"You come of a wealthy family?" he asked at last.

46

Colin smiled but made no answer.

"Come, I have told you that you had better answer!"

"If you are thinking of ransom, they will pay more for me whole than in little pieces," said Colin.

"That is likely. Well, you will write a letter to them and tell them that—but we will fix the amount of your ransom after further discussion. Tell me what your father does for a living. He is wealthy?"

Again Colin smiled without answering, and an angry growl rose from the crowd of men.

"A little persuasion, eh?" smiled the Black Pirate. "A lighted match between the fingers. Such a little persuasion after all! Come—bring a match, someone!"

"Untie his hands," shouted one of the watchers, and rough hands cut the rope and wrenched his stiffened arms round. Colin nearly fainted with the pain in his shoulder, but managed to restrain a cry. His hands were seized and the match was approaching when a sudden diversion called all attention away from him in an instant.

A man rushed on to the plateau shouting and panting. What he was saying Colin could not distinguish, but a fierce medley of voices took up the tale, and odd words came to him.

"An army—"

"White men—"

"Foreign devils—"

"Marching on this place—"

"Yes, with guns—many guns—terrible guns!"

47

Then the voice of the Black Pirate rose above the rest.

"Tie the prisoner hand and foot and leave him. And come you all to me. We will settle this affair and return to our sport afterwards."

Once more Colin was bound and flung down under the lee of a big rock, while the bandits gathered round their chief for their instructions in the emergency which had apparently come upon them.

Chapter 6

AMBUSHED!

FOR two days the Naval landing party marched in the most correct style inland, Their motorboat had landed them at a point some distance up river, and then the coolie who was leading them struck northwards. Jack Hawkins had his scouts out, and marched with the utmost caution. And never, during those two days, did they meet a single soul.

"How far are we now from the stronghold?" asked Jack as they made camp that evening.

Petty Officer Hardbake inquired from the coolie, and returned with the information that another day's good, hard marching would bring them within sight of the mountain in which it was located.

"Well, we haven't met anyone so far. You'd think he'd have some men out somewhere. What do you think, Hardbake? Do you think he's decamped?"

"I wouldn't go so far as to say that, sir."

"Well, shouldn't we have come across some burned-out villages or something if he were operating in these parts?"

"If there was any villages here for 'im to burn out, sir. But, as it is, it's pretty deserted, if you see what I mean."

"I think we're on the wrong track," said Jack moodily. "I don't think he's here at all."

The midshipman was wrong. At that moment

his very words were being listened to by a man who had seen from afar the glint of the setting sun on a fixed bayonet and who had come along to see what it was all about. He had wormed his way between the unsuspecting sentries, taking advantage of every bush and stone, every patch of shadow and rock, taking a good time to reach a place where he could see and overhear, but reaching it nevertheless.

Now he sat up in a leafy tree and listened, putting to good account the scraps of English he had learned in the alleys of Shanghai. He could not understand much of what was said, but he did understand when Petty Officer Hardbake asked the coolie how far it was to this Black Pirate of his, and he also understood the coolie's answer. He sat quietly in the tree until it was quite dark, and then slid down, as silently as a snake, and wormed his way past the sentries and into the open country again.

Being a hardy scoundrel, and not a file of naval ratings burdened with equipment, weapons and stores, he made very good time throughout the night until he reached the spot from which the mountain could be seen. With very few halts he trotted on throughout the day, and at last arrived after darkness had fallen to find the Black Pirate engaged with a prisoner.

But of all this Jack and his party had no idea. They roused and ate a good meal the following morning, and set off at a swinging pace on the last lap but one of their journey.

"I can't see the mountain yet," complained

Jack, staring about him as much as the shaggy country would permit.

"Little bit farther on, I guess, sir," said Hardbake imperturbably.

"It's as empty and deserted as the palm of my hand," said Jack, who was pining for a spot of action.

Hardbake did not reply immediately, and Jack looked at him inquiringly.

"No sir, nothing wrong—nothing wrong, exactly, sir. But I don't feel comfortable all of a sudden."

"What do you mean? Mosquitoes?"

"No sir, no. I can't put a word to it exactly, but there's somethink I don't like somewheres!"

"Getting nervous?" chuckled Jack, but he loosened his revolver in its webbing holster.

"Yes sir, that's it. Nervous. That's what I am at this moment. I dunno what it is, sir, but I smell trouble."

"The scouts haven't reported anything amiss," said Jack, trying not to feel put out.

"No sir, they 'aven't. I think, if you'll allow me, I'll go an' take a look at them scouts. Not exactly used to the country, some of 'em. I wouldn't like 'em to come to no 'arm."

"Very good, Petty Officer," nodded Jack, and Hardbake disappeared into the undergrowth at a trot.

Jack called his men to attention and told them to keep their eyes skinned. They would soon be entering a little rocky defile and he half thought of sending a couple of men round, before entering it, to make sure that the cliffs on either side were as deserted as they appeared to be. But he remembered in time that his scouts would have seen to that. That was what they were for. And they had sent back no warning. Jack and his men marched on.

They were well into the defile when, without warning, a horde of shrieking demons leaped from the cliffs on either side. landing clean on top of the marching sailors. There was no time to unship the machine guns nor to get the Brens into action. It was knife and fist work, with clinging yellow bandits on shoulder and back. And it was all over in a matter of minutes. Jack's meagre dozen was swamped by nearly thirty pirates, and although each man fought like a tiger, there could be only one end to it.

Jack himself was hit on the head before he could fire one shot from his revolver, and only recovered consciousness to find himself slung by wrists and ankles from a pole, in the middle of a marching crowd of jubilant ruffians.

For hours the march went on. Jack lost consciousness again, recovered for a short time, and fainted once more. The pain in his tethered wrists and ankles was terrible and he was hard put to it not to groan. The knock on the head had scattered his wits somewhat, and he was not at all sure what had happened. But as night came on the plateau was reached and the prisoners thrown down to recover as best they might, and in the coolness and welcome relief from the pain of transit, Jack found himself able to think again.

They had walked into a trap, that much was sure. But how was it that the scouts had not warned them? His mind roved fruitlessly round and round this question, and at last he abandoned it to consider his present position.

All around him lay his men. He could not see how many there were, and his heart chilled as he wondered how many had been killed in the fighting. They had started out fourteen strong—a dozen ratings, the petty officer and himself. And now, how many were there? Two of the ratings had gone ahead as scouts, of course, and Hardbake had gone to find them. So that left eleven. Were there eleven men lying there? He tried to see, but found that he could not move.

In the distance he could see a big fire burning, and the pirates—there seemed to be myriads of them—were shouting and carousing around it. Apparently a great feast of victory was going on, and from the noise Jack guessed that most of the ruffians would be dead drunk before the night was out.

Suddenly one of the pirates detached himself from the crowd and staggered towards them.

"Pretend to be still unconscious," hissed Jack, not knowing whether any of his men were sufficiently conscious to hear him or not. He closed his eyes and lay still, and the man, carrying a blazing brand, staggered up to him.

"Not awake yet, my little turkey?" hiccupped the man, swaying to and fro. "Come—wake up. There is a feast for you. Wake up and join in!"

Jack lay still and silent, and, growling a curse, the man staggered off. Then a cautious voice spoke from behind the midshipman.

"What did he mean about a feast, sir? I could do with a drink myself."

"Is that Stacey?" Jack asked eagerly, in a low voice.

"Yes sir."

"Are you all right?"

"A bit knocked about sir, but that's all. I don't know as there's any bones broken."

"That's good."

"What about yourself, sir?"

"Just the same. A crack on the head, I should judge by the way it's aching. And my wrists and ankles are pretty sore—if not dislocated. Gosh, what a trip that was!"

"It was, sir. You think there's no chance of a drink, sir?"

"None, I'm afraid. His idea of a feast isn't quite ours. He intends us to take the part of unwilling entertainers, I imagine. You keep your eyes shut, and sham dead as long as you can!"

"Cor! You think they mean to torture us, sir?"

"I shouldn't be surprised."

"Look out, sir! Here comes another of 'em."

This time it was the Black Pirate himself who came to look at them, accompanied by two or three of his gang. Jack took a look at him out of half-closed eyes, and thought he had never seen a more terrifying-looking scoundrel. He remem-

54

bered what Lieutenant Burgoyne had told him of his chances if he were captured, and once again wished with all his heart that he had obeyed the impulse to search the cliffs above the defile before he led his men into it.

"I should like to question these men," said the Black Pirate, but Jack could not understand his words.

"Why not?" asked one of the gang.

"The men are too drunk, and perhaps it would be better to wait until they are all conscious," was the reply.

"True, they sleep soundly!"

"You have not brought me dead men, I hope?" asked the leader venomously. He bent down and ran his hand over Jack's face and neck. "No, he is warm. He is not dead. I wonder if he is shamming?" A rough finger lifted the midshipman's eyelid, and Jack tensed himself not to flinch. If the Pirate had not partaken so thoroughly of the intoxicating liquor that was the main part of their feast of victory he must have noticed the movement, but as it was he was satisfied. "He sleeps," he said with an oath. "We will have our sport to-morrow."

The unsteady footsteps went away, and presently Jack opened his eyes and saw that they were once more alone.

"It's all right, Stacey," he muttered.

"What did he do, sir?"

"Just looked to see if I were awake. I think I foxed him all right."

"What did he say, sir?"

55

"I wish I knew! I don't understand their lingo, I'm afraid. Hardbake is the man for that. By the way, is the Petty Officer here? Did they get him too?"

"I dunno, sir."

"Pass the word back. See if anyone knows anything about him."

The muttered question went round the men, to those who were in full possession of their faculties at any rate, but there was no response. No one knew anything about the Petty Officer. Some thought they had seen him just before the surprise attack, but most of them said that they had not seen him for some time. There seemed to be good reason to suppose that he had escaped, and Jack's spirits suddenly rose.

"If he got away, men, there's a chance for us. He'll go back to the ship and get help, and the Captain'll bring a landing party ashore to rescue us."

"Maybe, with luck, they'll be in time to give us Christian burial," said a mournful voice out of the darkness.

"I shouldn't call that luck, exactly," said Jack.

"I've heard about these Chinks," said another man. "And I reckon if you die quick it's considered luck!"

"You're right, chum. We've had it!" said Leading Seaman Stacey.

"Well, I ain't a-goin' to lie down an' die, not for nobody," said Seaman Binns sturdily. "I reckon if we can stop alive long enough, we'll git rescued. Don't you think so, sir?"

"I hope so," said Jack.

"Besides, we dunno as they use torture," said an optimistic individual. "I don't think as they do, not in these days."

"I'm afraid you're wrong," said an unfamiliar voice. "They do!"

Chapter 7

COMRADES IN MISFORTUNE

"WHO spoke then?" asked Jack sharply.

"I'm a prisoner too, but I've been in their hands two days longer than you have," was the reply given in a weary voice.

"And they've tortured you?"

"Yes."

"What for?"

"They want me to answer some questions."

"What about?"

"Oh—my father, and so on."

"Did they—what did they do?"

"Nothing much—yet. My hands are burned a bit. But they've got a fine programme mapped out for the future!"

"And where do we come in?" asked Leading Seaman Stacey.

"I'm afraid he's going to question you to-morrow."

"How do you know?" asked several voices breathlessly.

"I heard what he said when he came to look at you. You were very wise to pretend not to be conscious!"

"What sort of things is he likely to want to know?" asked Jack slowly.

"Well, his main idea is to hold people to ransom. Those who obviously can't pay will be tortured to death to provide his men with sport. Their idea of sport!"

"What a pleasant plan!" ejaculated a seaman.

"I could bluff him that a ransom would be paid for us all in a body, or not at all," said Jack, thinking hard.

"Possibly."

"And keep him guessing until the punitive expedition arrives."

"And as soon as his spies bring news of the approach of the expedition, of course, you'd be for it! You understand that?"

"There's always the possibility of escape," muttered Jack.

"I see none at the moment. Are you tied?"

"Wrists and ankles," said Jack laconically.

"So am I."

"What about your hands?"

"What about them?"

"Well, didn't you say they were burned? Are they bandaged, or anything?"

"No. I've a bullet wound in my shoulder, too. I managed to pad it with my handkerchief, but it's stuck to that and to my blouse too. No, they don't go in for Red Cross work up here."

"But—I say! A bullet wound in your shoulder? Does it throb?"

"No, I don't think it's septic or anything. It's my hands that are most painful. I think, actually, the shoulder is healing up all right."

"Did you put iodine on it?"

A short laugh was the only answer, and there was silence for a little while.

"So there doesn't seem much chance of escape," said Colin at last. "And believe me, if I could think of one I'd be the happiest fellow on earth!"

"That goes for all of us," said Jack.

"I think I've an added reason for wanting to get free. My father lives three or four days' journey from here, and yesterday I heard the scoundrels discussing pushing their expedition in that direction when they've finished with us. They've been through all the north bank of the river, and a week's journey to the west. They know there's nothing eastwards, between them and the sea. But the south bank they haven't explored much yet. They were scouting about there when they caught me and murdered my companion, as a matter of fact. And if they get to our village they'll burn it and kill every soul in it, as they always do. And I can't warn them of their danger!"

There was another long silence. Jack was thinking that the possible plight of the village was less important to him than the fate of his men and of himself, but he supposed that if the lad's father were in the village he might feel differently. Then light broke on him.

"Are they torturing you to find out where your father is?"

"More or less, yes."

"And you won't tell them?"

"How can I?"

"Gosh, that's awful! But can't you spin them a yarn?"

"No, I can't do that."

"What do you mean? Tell them that he's a

millionaire in Chicago and will pay a fortune to get you safely back again."

"Well, quite apart from the fact that it isn't true, what would be the use of it? What happens when the fortune doesn't arrive?"

"Well—you'd have more time to plan an escape."

"Anything might happen," put in Stacey encouragingly. "You can say as we're all your brothers, an' the old man'll pay a million for each of us."

"I'm sorry. I can't. And it wouldn't be any use if I could."

"It would make time," said Jack restlessly. "A good thumping yarn, properly told—why not?"

"If you think it's all right, you can do it. But I can't."

"Are you telling me that you'd rather be tortured than spin a yarn to this pirate chap?"

"It isn't a question of what I'd rather do. I can't lie, and that's that."

"I don't get you," said Jack in astonishment. "Where's the harm?"

"You see no harm in lying?"

"Oh, come off it! In ordinary circumstances I wouldn't lie—I think it's a beastly habit. I think I'm as truthful in ordinary life as most people. It wasn't encouraged at home—lying, I mean. Dad was rather hot on it. But now —at a time like this—surely any means are justifiable?"

"I don't see it that way. If a thing's wrong, it's wrong, and that's all there is to it."

"I think you're mad!" Jack said, and he really did.

"He's right," said Binns, the seaman, hesitantly.

"Thank you, whoever you are," said Colin. "And there's this, too. That black villain knows what the white man stands for—you know what I mean—truth and honesty and courage. And Christianity. I should have put that first, really. But if I lie to save my own skin—well, I let everything down, don't I?"

"Pertic'larly Christianity," said Binns.

"Yes but—" began Jack, but fell silent.

"I don't want to seem to be self-righteous," said Colin slowly, "but my father is a missionary, and I'm following him in his profession. And how could I teach truth to the heathen if I'd saved my life by a lie?"

"Would anyone know?" muttered Jack.

"God would know."

"Well, what's God going to do to get you out of this mess?" asked Jack harshly. "You say He knows. What's He going to do about it?"

Colin was silent for a moment, and when he spoke again his voice was stronger and more cheerful.

"I don't know, but He'll do something! I think I'd rather forgotten Whom it is that I serve, lying here being sorry for myself because my hands were hurting, and worrying about the people at home. Thanks for reminding me. It's not my responsibility. Our Father will look after them, and me too. I've only got to be faithful to my trust, and He is always faithful."

"That sounds very nice—for you!" grunted Jack. "What about us?"

"Well, He cares for you just as much as He cares for me. Put yourself in His hands and He'll look out for you."

"Ah, I wouldn't say that," said Jack with an uneasy laugh. "How could He care as much for me, for instance, as He does for you? I'm not a bad sort of chap, but I'm not a missionary and don't intend to be one. I can't say I go in for that sort of thing much."

"Our Heavenly Father has no favourites," said Colin slowly. "I wish Dad were here—he can put things better than I can—he'd show you just what I mean. But God has no favourites. He loves all his children. The greatest proof of God's love is that He sent His son to be the Saviour of all. He put our sins on Him, but it's up to us whether we believe this for ourselves or not. Look now—the sun shines on you just as brightly as it shines on me, and the rain wets me just as much as it wets you. It works the other way round, somehow. I do wish I could be clear, because it does seem so important when we may all be dead to-morrow! Look at it like this—He gives freely to everyone, but it's up to you whether you take it or not. All the richness of the earth, our food and that, it comes from Him, but it's up to us whether we realize that and thank Him or not."

"But what good does it do you?" asked Jack.

"Well—" Colin gave a little stifled laugh. "What good does it do you anyway to be grateful for a gift? It isn't that. You just *are* grateful, if you realize it, aren't you?"

"I suppose so," grunted Jack. "But how does that help us out of this mess?"

"Ah—that's different. His gifts are given to everyone, but His help can only reach you if you ask for it."

"You mean if I ask for help now I'm as likely to get it as you, who've been on His side all your life? That isn't fair!"

"Well, if I don't mind, I don't see what you have to grumble at! And—look here—you can't dictate to God! You can't tell Him how and when you want to be rescued. If you get the right idea of yourself as one of millions and millions of little people, and Him as the King and Creator of the universe, you'll understand that. I don't suppose you tell one of your own admirals just how and when you want things done—so how much less can you do so to God, once you realize Who He is!"

Jack moved uneasily in his bonds, but said nothing.

"I get that, sir," said Leading Seaman Stacey. "But what can we do?"

"You'll have to say—and mean—that whatever He sends you'll take with a good heart," said Colin slowly. "And ask for His help and strength. It'll come, if you do, through the power of His Holy Spirit. And remember that if you're really on His side, nothing much can happen to you. He'll be with you all the way. After all, even death is nothing if He is there."

"That's right, sir," said Binns eagerly. "I
don't want to die, not much. There's plenty I
want to do before that comes. But I'm not afraid.
I know Whom I trust and I know where I'm
goin', because He said so. See?"

"You've got it," said Colin.

"I don't fancy torture much," Binns went on
rather ruefully, "but I reckon I can stand it with
His help."

"That's the spirit!" Colin said. "Christ
suffered too, torture and death. He knows all
about it and that's how He can give us the
strength we need. He understands. What hurts
us, hurts Him too—He's with us in it all. And
He'll help us to win, as He won, whether in life
or death."

"Well, I'll do my bit. I hope He does His!"
said Stacey rather doubtfully.

"The most important part of your bit is trusting
Him," said Colin.

"Well, I suppose I can manage that too."

"What I can't get straight is this," said Jack.
"If I—er—do what you say, and God gets us out
of this somehow, do I have to chuck the Navy and
be a missionary for the rest of my life?"

"You wouldn't want to?" asked Colin.

"I'd hate it!" said Jack emphatically.

"But would you do it?"

"If I had to, of course. Is that what it means?
I'd better know what's expected of me. I'd do
it, of course, to get my men and myself out of this
mess. You—He could depend on me to keep my
side of the bargain, even if it's that."

"You can't bargain with God. You can only make your submission and you can tell Him then, as freely as you could your earthly father, what you hope and what you fear. But you can't bargain. You must take what He sends. But I don't think He'd want you to chuck the Navy. You'll know all right. He'll make it clear. Well —what about it? Will you come into line?"

"O.K." said Jack abruptly. "He wins!"

A quiet murmur of agreement came from the crowd of bound men, and Colin's heart was uplifted in a surge of gratitude that God had allowed him to be of use.

"If I die to-morrow," he thought to himself, "I've been able to do something! And I'll go in good company!"

Chapter 8

A RESCUE

THE night was very quiet. After the momentous words had been spoken and Jack had announced his decision to "come into line", everyone kept silence. Jack himself was wondering exactly what he had let himself in for. He knew very little about religion and had generally allowed his mind to wander at will during Divisions, or any other Naval occasion when the Christian faith is brought to the attention of a ship's company. Now he realized that he must think about it, and think hard. He had taken on something on the word of a fellow whom, actually, he had never seen although he knew instinctively from his voice that he could be trusted. What was his name? He did not know. There had been no introductions. They were all in the same boat, all prisoners of a bloodthirsty pirate, all hurt in some way or another, and all without any real hope of a rescue. That was their position, in plain language. In a very short time they would all probably be dead. Well!

And then this nameless chap had started talking about God. What had he said? Jack could not remember. But whatever it was, it had suddenly induced in him this desire to "come into line" What had he meant by it?

For the first time in his life Jack Hawkins began really and honestly to think about God. Who was God? Well, this chap had called him King and Creator of the world. Jack supposed that He was just that. After all, someone had created the world; such an amazing thing could not have happened by accident. Very well then: the person, whoever he was, who had created it must be called God.

And King? Well, that followed. Having created the world, made it out of nothing, it surely followed that God had a right to be obeyed by the things that He had made. Jack felt ashamed of the years in which he had failed in obedience. A Naval man knows all about obedience. He obeys his officers, and knows that they, too, obey others higher than themselves. And the highest of all obey the king. And he, supposed Jack, obeys God, so everyone obeys someone.

And the reason for that obedience? Jack knew the answer to that too. It is for the good of the ship and the ship's company that strict obedience is enforced, not for the satisfaction and amusement of the captain. He knew, as all sailors know, that there can only be one captain in a ship, and that the safety and honour of the ship and her crew depend on him. If his commands are carried out in a slack and slovenly manner, then everyone suffers. All are depending on each other for their safety and comfort, and all look to the captain to see to it that this dependence is not betrayed.

And so, thought Jack in the black stillness of that night, so it is in the world. God is the Captain. The other fellow had spoken of Him as a Father, but Jack preferred to own Him as Captain. It was a word he knew and understood. Well, if everyone in the world obeyed God as the members of the crew of a happy ship obeyed their captain, what a different place the world would be! Jack might not know very much about religion, but commonsense and some early memories told him that such things as kindness, truthfulness, honesty and courage were virtues encouraged by God.

His mind turned to the Son of God Who had shown that such a life was possible and Who, according to this nameless speaker in the dark, would stand by a chap in the difficult times. He had fought evil and had died, but, Jack remembered, that wasn't the end. In the end He had defeated death and evil. He was alive still, and ready to help. It was new and strange, but he knew in his heart that it was true.

Well, he had promised to "come into line". That meant that he had joined the ship's company of the Heavenly Captain. It was up to him now to report for duty, and, having got his orders, to carry them out. And if God did get them out of this mess alive it would be up to him, of course, to read up his new King's Regulations, and find out a bit more about Him. And if they died to-morrow—well, he was surprised to find that the thought no longer brought a sick feeling to his heart. Funny thing—he wasn't frightened at all! In fact, he was sleepy. If anyone had told him that he could close his eyes and go to sleep in that uncomfortable position and with that terrifying fate hanging over him, he would not have believed it. But there it was; his eyes were closing. His Captain was in command, and all he had to do was to wait for his orders. He slept.

To the rest of his little band sleep came too. All were more or less hurt, some severely, but all had listened eagerly to the talk of the chap with the burned hands, as they thought of Colin among themselves. And each, in his own way, thought the matter out as Jack had done, and each felt relieved and peaceful when he had done so.

The pirates slept too, but theirs was the heavy slumber of drunkenness. Lying round their dying fire, or heaped on one another in the various caves and rocky shelters that ringed the plateau, they snored in happy oblivion. The fire sank lower and lower and the night was very dark.

Jack woke with a start as a hand was placed over his mouth. For a second or two his senses whirled wildly and he could not remember either where he was or what had happened. Then he heard a voice whispering urgently in his ear, and his brain steadied. He remembered everything.

"Are you all right, sir? This is Petty Officer Hardbake, sir. Will you nod if you're all right sir? I'm afraid to take me 'and away in case you shouts out or somethink, not bein' properly awake."

Jack managed to nod, and the hand was cautiously removed. It was so dark that it was quite impossible to see the owner of the hand, but it was easy to recognize the owner of that voice.

"Sure you're all right, sir?"

"Yes, I'm all right, Petty Officer. Tied up like a trussed chicken, though."

"I'll git you free in a jiffy, sir." A knife cut through the ropes as though they had been cotton and Jack tried to move his stiffened limbs.

"Crumbs! It hurts!" he muttered.

"Ah, it will, sir. Rub your wrists, sir, an' as soon as you can, git some o' the chaps free like I done you. Don't fergit as a chap wakened sharp like is inclined to shout, will you, sir?"

"I'll remember," whispered Jack, and very soon was able to get busy.

At last the task was done, but a sad state of affairs now revealed itself. None of them was unwounded, and three men were definitely too badly hurt to be able to walk.

"You better leave us, sir," muttered one man, Curly Robins by name.

"Not likely!" said Jack. "We'll carry you, don't you worry. Either we all go or none of us do, I'll tell you that!"

"You leave us, sir," insisted another of the wounded men, Pincher Martin. "We should only be a drag on you. You want to git away fast, you do. We can only die once!"

"You're not dying this trip! Come along chaps—I'm not wounded, and Curly—you can lean on me."

"Someone can lean on me," said Colin quietly.

"Eh? Who's that?" ejaculated the Petty Officer.

"A friend of mine," said Jack. "Right—but are you sure your hands will let you?"

"They're all right. And I think I can show you the way. You were all unconscious more or less as you came up, but I was all there. I know the way down."

"I know the way back to the ship," said Petty Officer Hardbake, slipping his arms round one of the wounded men and heaving him up on to his back. "This way, sir." And he started off, cat-footed in the darkness, down the side of the hill.

It was slow going. The darkness made it necessary to feel for every step, and in every man's mind was the thought that the night was passing, and with the dawn their enemies would discover their escape and be after them. But no one spoke of this; each man concealed his sufferings as the jerks and stumbles hurt his wounds, and the sorely hurt tried not to lean too heavily on the shoulders of those who were helping them.

"Spell-o," said Petty Officer Hardbake suddenly, and the tired men sat down thankfully. "Now sir, we're well away from that place, what's the plan?"

"To get back to the ship with all speed," said Jack. "I suppose, by the way, you didn't manage to find any of our weapons?"

"No sir. I snooped about a good bit, but I couldn't come nigh 'em. I reckon they're all away in the back o' one o' them caves, but to git at 'em we'd have to walk right over the pirates themselves, an' I didn't reckon that would be safe, somehow."

"I know where the machine guns are, Mr. Hardbake," said Stacey doiefully.

"Where's that, then?"

"They chucked 'em over a cliff into a river. I seed 'em myself. They was muckin' about with 'em, an' then they chucks 'em over. Couldn't think how they worked, I suppose. Well, they're gone, any old how."

"Too bad," said Jack. "But we couldn't have carried them. It's all we can do to get ourselves away, let alone guns and ammunition. No, I only hoped that perhaps my pistol had turned up, but it doesn't matter. We should be easy meat in a scrap, so all we can do is to beat it."

"You can take my pistol sir, an' welcome," said the Petty Officer instantly.

"No, Hardbake, you keep it. I couldn't hit a haystack in my present condition. Well—shall we carry on?"

"May I make a suggestion?" asked Colin.

"Surely! Your suggestions turn out to be good ones, I believe, eh?"

"I'm very glad you think so. Well, it's this. You want to get back to your ship, and I want to get back to my father and the village—"

"I'd forgotten that!" Jack said in consternation.

"What's that, sir?" asked Hardbake instantly.

"Why—oh, what is your name? Mine's Hawkins—Jack Hawkins. So far you're only a voice, but you ought to have a name."

"Oh yes, I've got a name all right. Colin Wedderburn."

"Thank you, sir," said Petty Officer Hardbake.

"Well," said Jack, "Mr. Wedderburn's father is in a village three days' journey from here, roughly, and the Black Pirate means to go and burn it down shortly."

"H'm!" said the Petty Officer.

"But I think we ought to stop him, don't you?"

"I think we ought to git our wounded back to the ship, an' git another landin' party together to deal with this pirate, sir. I think that's our dooty, if I may say so."

"I think I can help you there," said Colin. "On the way here we passed the pirate's junk, and as far as I could see, it was fairly lightly held. In fact, I only saw one sentry, though there may have been others—"

"I say!" said Jack.

"So why don't you take the junk and sail down to your ship, and bring up a landing party to the rescue of the village?"

"That's the idea, sir!" cried Hardbake jubilantly, smacking his thigh in triumph.

"Well, lead us to the junk," said Jack. "I must admit it sounds tempting. The first step is to take it; after we've done that we can discuss the next one."

And so, hope once more burning brightly in all their hearts, they began the difficult descent of the mountain. But it was getting easier all the time. The first stiffness had long worn off, and even the wounded were feeling the better for action. The seriously hurt men were not so good, and Curly was now being carried by two of his comrades, while Colin gave a shoulder to

74

help Jack with Pincher.   Hardbake said he
needed no help with his burden, and indeed,
seemed as fresh as though he had not spent the
whole of the night in difficult circumstances.

When the first grey light of dawn made their
task plain they put on more speed, almost fearing
to look behind them in case they should find they
had not come as far as they had hoped or that the
shaggy head of a bandit should appear behind a
rifle at their elbow.   But they had indeed made
very good time, and before very long Colin was
able to show them that he had been right in
thinking that he knew the way.

"There's the river," he said, pointing.   "And
there's the junk among the reeds."

Chapter 9

A FORLORN HOPE

"WE'D better make a plan of campaign," said
Jack, staring at the masts of the junk, which was
all that they could see of her from where they
stood.

"That's right, sir," said Petty Officer Hardbake.
"We dunno how many there are of 'em aboard,
do we?"

"I can find that out," said Colin.

They all looked at him.

"Of course—I'd forgotten. You understand
their lingo," said Jack.

"And I'm wearing Chinese kit," said Colin.
"At a distance he wouldn't be able to tell me from
one of the bandits."

"What do you propose to do?" asked Jack.

"Go down and hail him. I'll find out how
many there are aboard, and let you know."

"In the meantime, while you're engaging him
in conversation we could work round to take
them in the rear," said Jack.

"It would mean swimming. She's moored in
midstream. And if there are more than the one
sentry, one of the others might see you."

"We could get pretty near unseen, under cover
of the reeds," said Jack.

"And there's a sampan down there—at least,
there was. That would help."

"I suggest we go down and make our disposi-
tions. Then you hail the chap and find out their

numbers. Then couldn't you give us a whistle as a signal?"

"Right," agreed Colin. "If I whistle once it means there's only the one man there. If twice, two. And if I give three whistles it means more than two but I don't know how many."

"We'll leave the three wounded men here," said Jack, meaning the three seriously wounded men, for all were hurt in some way or another. "Now, do any of the rest of you feel unequal to an attack on the junk?"

A short, fierce laugh was the only answer. Not one of them would have stayed out of that fight as long as they had feet to stand on and hands to use. Jack laughed too.

"A fine lot of cripples we are to be attacking anything! Never mind. Let's go. As for you three—" he paused as he tried to think what word of comfort he could give to the three desperately wounded men, whose wounds had not even been attended to. "Well, you know as well as I do what it means. If we don't come back—"

"I know sir. Don't you worry! You can't do no more than your best," said Pincher Martin with a pale grin.

"Could you put a bit o' rag round my side, sir before you go?" asked Curly faintly. "It's started bleedin' again."

"We must make time for that," said Jack, and knelt down by the man's side. A rough and ready first aid was applied, and to the other two men as well, and then the little expedition set off.

"I've been meaning to ask—what about our

scouts, Petty Officer?" asked Jack as they went forward.

"Never contacted 'em at all, sir. I reckon the bandits bumped 'em orf before 'and, so to speak. I looked around an' I looked around, an' then I 'eard the goin's on when you was attacked. I came forward cautious to see if there was any-think I could do, but it was all over before I got within range. If I'd started shootin' then it wouldn't ha' done no good. It was about fifty to one. I reckoned I'd do better to lay low an' trust to the everlastin' luck o' the British Navy to show me when to intervene."

"You certainly chose a good moment. Well— we ought to find that sampan soon if our friend's right about it being here."

They searched among the reeds, and presently found the dilapidated craft insecurely moored to a rotting stump. Jack got in.

"Not too seaworthy, Petty Officer!"

"Mustn't grumble, sir! With a bit o' luck mebbe she'll just take us to our objective."

"Well—all aboard, then."

They crowded in, nine desperate men with but one pistol between them to take a craft that might be full of pirates. One of the seamen took the big oar and worked them slowly towards the fringe of the reeds.

"Steady!" Jack said, parting the tall reeds and staring across at the junk. "I think we can get nearer if we go upstream a bit. The creek curves just there."

Carefully they moved on, the men helping by

pulling at the reeds as they passed. Great was Jack's joy when he found that the junk was actually moored to a spit of land that jutted out from the farther bank, and that the reeds slightly above them filled the creek entirely, affording all the cover they wanted.

' Excellent!" said Jack as they manœuvred into position. Now I wonder how long that chap's going to be?"

Meanwhile Colin was carrying out his part of the business. He sauntered down to the water's edge whistling a song that he remembered hearing the coolies sing in days gone by. He stood on the little cleared space where his captors had landed him previously, and, hollowing his hands about his mouth, hailed the junk with a shout.

A gun barrel appeared over the side of the deck, followed by a matted head.

"What do you want?" shouted the sentry.

"How goes it?" asked Colin amiably, squatting down on the beach in coolie fashion.

"All is well. Where do you come from?"

"Up yonder," said Colin with a casual wave of the hand behind him. "Great doings last night," he added.

"What doings?"

"An army of foreign devils captured and brought in for questioning. And such a feast!"

"Ah!" said the man enviously. "Some people have all the luck!"

"The fun isn't over yet," said Colin. "When does your relief come? You may see some of it yet."

"My relief should have been here last night," said the sentry sourly.

"Ah, he forgot, with all the fun going on. Too bad!" Colin moved along the strand a little, scraping the mud as if looking for shell-fish.

"I've a good mind to go and wake him up!" said the man truculently.

"Are you alone there?" asked Colin idly.

"Of course not. Three of us, as usual. Who are you, not to know that?"

"What business is it of mine?" asked Colin, squatting down again.

The man walked up and down for a minute or two, and then shouted for his companions, who came tumbling up from below. He told them the news and a furious argument developed. It was clear that he wanted to go and join in the fun with the prisoners, and wanted the other two to stay behind and guard the junk. It was equally clear that the other two saw matters in quite a different light. At last it was suggested that they should draw lots, and this was done. But the lot to stay behind fell on the sentry who had talked with Colin, and he protested vehemently that whoever stayed behind it was his privilege to go, and the argument started all over again.

Colin squatted on the shore, moving from time to time nearer the reeds pawing over the mud and taking no apparent notice of the discussion aboard the junk. Jack and his party, watching from a hidden spot so near that they could hear the voice raised in heated argument, wondered what it was all about.

"What's going on, Hardbake?" he asked. "Can you make out at all?"

"Far as I can judge, sir, that Mr. Wedderburn has told 'em there's some fun goin' on up at the camp, an' they all want to go an' join in."

"That's a good idea!" Jack ejaculated. "I'm as game as any man for a fight, but if we can take this junk without a scrap, I think it won't do us any harm."

"You're right, sir," said the Petty Officer.

"Golly!" interrupted Binns suddenly. "They're goin'!"

"So they are!" said Jack excitedly. "Jolly good show!"

"What about Pincher and them, sir?" asked Binns urgently. "When them chaps go up to the place, they'll pass right by 'em!"

"That is so!" Jack was thunderstruck. "Petty Officer—if you take two men with you, do you think you could move them out of sight before the bandits get there?"

"I could try, sir. An' if I can't, I got me pistol," said Hardbake grimly.

"Back to the shore then, lads," said Jack, and the old sampan shifted through the reeds at a pace it had never known before. It was essential that the Petty Officer and his two men should get ashore before the pirates, and this they managed to do. Leaping on to dry land, they ran, doubling and crouching, among the rocks and bushes, until they reached the spot where their companions were lying.

Petty Officer Hardbake took in the possibilities of the place with a single glance.

"Be'ind that there rock," he said. "They won't be a-lookin' for us—they'll be that anxious to get up an' see the fun. Handsomely now—handsomely! Don't jar the poor chaps. There—that's right."

The bandits, still arguing furiously as to who should go, crowded into their boat and rowed to the shore. There they began to fight, shouting and screaming with fury, until one of them had a clever idea.

"Make the coolie stay and watch the junk!" he shouted. "He can have my gun. Coolie—can you shoot?"

"Duck—yes," said Colin.

"Not duck. Men. Foreign devils."

"Where?" cried Colin, looking amazed.

"Fool! If the foreign devils come you must shoot them. You will stay here and watch the junk while we go and send the relief down. And if the foreign devils come you will shoot them."

Colin laughed and scratched in the mud.

"I can shoot," he said. "Leave the gun."

The gun was thrown down and the men began to hasten up the hill. After a moment or two Colin stood up to watch their progress, and it was then that he remembered the three hurt men. His face paled. He had delivered them into the enemy's hands! He ran and picked up the gun as well as his burned hands would allow. It was loaded, and he stood with it in his arms, waiting.

They were approaching the place now. If they stopped he would shoot.

But they did not stop. To his great perplexity they went straight on, as if there were nothing there. When they were mere dots on the hillside, climbing nimbly, he got into the boat and paddled himself over to the junk.

Jack had taken the sampan back to its position near the mud spit and was waiting impatiently for the signal. Then he saw Colin coming out to the junk, and hailed him.

"Shall we board?"

"Yes. They've gone."

"Splendid work!" The sampan shot forward, and, running along the spit of land, Jack and his companions swarmed up on to the craft, leaving Stacey making the sampan fast below.

"Did you think of the wounded?" asked Colin as Jack, his face radiant with delight, met him on the deck.

"Rather! Hardbake went back to move them out of sight."

"Oh, good! I'm sorry to say I forgot them until the men started off, and then I was all ready to shoot them with this old iron if they'd found them. If I could have hit them!" he added ruefully.

"Your hands!" said Jack, catching sight of them. "Whew! They ought to have some attention."

"Yes, I think they ought. I might be of some use if they were cleaned and tied up, but I can't do much with them as it is. But let's get the wounded aboard first, shall we? I'd feel happier if we were all together."

"Right," said Jack, and gave orders for the wounded men to be brought down and loaded into the sampan. Meanwhile he and Colin cleared a shaded spot on the deck where they could lie, and then went on a tour of inspection of their new craft.

"Well, I suppose I could make shift to sail her, but I think Hardbake will know more about it than I do," said Jack, viewing the tangle of cordage and sails with some distaste.

"Here he comes," said Colin. "Well! That's the first step towards safety. We've got our ship."

Chapter 10

THE JUNK

"THERE are several things to be done," said Jack when all his crew were aboard, "and we must take them in order. We must attend to our wounds or they'll go septic. We must clear the boom from the river, and we must sail the junk downstream to the sea. Now it is possible that the pirates are even now searching for us. It is equally possible that they're still sleeping off their drunken stupor. But it's quite evident that the sooner we're out of here the better, so I'll say no more and we'll get busy. Mr. Hardbake, will you take Binns and Stacey—unless they want treatment?"

"No sir, I'm O.K., sir," chorused the two seamen.

"Binns 'as a cut arm an' Stacey 'ad a bash on the 'ead," put in another seaman.

"Well, 'tain't nothink," said Stacey angrily.

"Let me have a look," said Jack. "Ah—a lump as big as a duck's egg! But they couldn't get through that thick skull of yours, could they, Stacey? I think you're all right. Let's see your arm, Binns."

"It's tied up, sir. And it don't hurt."

"Right you are, then. Petty Officer—will you take these two men, find the boom, and clear it? I don't know what sort of boom it is nor how you're going to tackle it, but as I get the rest of the men patched up I'll send some down to help you."

"Ay, ay sir," said the Petty Officer, and he led his little party into the smaller boat and rowed off down the creek towards the river.

Then the task of the first aid was begun in earnest, and in very difficult circumstances. Naturally there was nothing aboard the junk that could be used for bandages or anything like that, but one or two of the emergency first-aid kits carried by the seamen had survived the looting of the pirates, and with some tearing up of underclothes the job was done.

The first lightly-wounded man was given the sentry's gun and told to keep watch. The second was sent below to get some sort of a fire going to boil up some water. After that things were easier, and one by one the bandaged heroes were sent either to some task or to join Petty Officer Hardbake.

From time to time Jack went himself to the landward side of the junk and stared towards the distant mountain. Everything looked very peaceful. He strained his eyes to see if the bandits were coming down to the attack, but there was no sign of any such thing. Only a warm, sunny morning, with birds singing above the river, and no sign of human life anywhere.

"I wonder why they don't come?" muttered Jack. "They must know by now that we've gone."

"Will the bandits have got up there yet?" wondered Colin.

"Hardly. I know they were going at a pretty good lick, but it's a long way. It took us most of the night to come down, anyway!"

86

"Yes, it took us some hours to get up, but the light wasn't good, and I was pretty tired. These chaps were making all haste to get there before the fun was over. I wish you could have seen them! More like mountain goats than men."

"Well, they'll be disappointed when they do get there!"

"I've just thought of something. I believe their going off like that is the best bit of luck we've had since your petty officer arrived last night. Do you realize, the first thing the Black Pirate will ask them is if they met anyone on their way up. They'll say no, and he'll conclude that we've gone in the other direction!"

"Of course!" cried Jack, laughing suddenly. "What a bit of luck! And by the time they search this sector, we'll have gone."

"I still think we'd better hurry," said Colin.

"You're right, of course. Well, I think that's the last of the cripples. What about you?"

"I don't quite know what you can do for me, except tie my hands up," said Colin.

Jack inspected the inflamed fingers with concern.

"They must be painful."

"They are. But as long as I can keep dirt out of them, I don't think we can do anything else."

"Oughtn't we to break these blisters?"

"Perhaps. Go ahead if you think so."

Jack did go ahead, and Colin agreed that the hands were not so painful after that had been done. Then Jack soaked some fairly clean cloth in boiled water and tied the hands up. They had no burn dressings and he could think of nothing else that would be helpful.

"What about your shoulder? Didn't you say there was a bullet in it?"

"Not in it. I think it went straight through. I don't think I'll have that touched, if you don't mind. It's quite comfortable, and I think it's healing quite nicely under the pad. If you start pulling it off, you'll start it bleeding again."

"Just as you like. It looks pretty messy, though."

"That's only the blood on my blouse."

"Right you are then. Well, I think I'll go and give Hardbake a hand. Will you stay aboard and keep a general eye on things? If you see anything you don't like, give a whistle and we'll come back right away."

"I will," said Colin, and Jack set off, taking with him the last remaining men who could do any sort of work, with the sole exception of the sentry.

Colin went over to the side of the junk and satisfied himself that nothing was happening on the mountainside. Then he saw that the wounded men were comfortable, and then he boiled some more water and set it to cool in case any of them wanted a drink. After that he began a systematic search for food and found plenty. Admittedly it was Chinese food, but he did not mind that, and he had an idea that if he prepared it appetizingly his companions would not mind it either.

And so, with frequent journeys to the deck to keep an eye on the mountain and the wounded,

Colin laboriously and with considerable difficulty began to prepare a meal in the galley. It was a long time since any of them had eaten.

Meanwhile the boom, a complicated system of rocks, bushes, bamboo poles and wire, was being patiently taken to pieces by Petty Officer Hardbake and his working party. Jack joined in with a will when he arrived, and, slipping off his torn and stained clothes, dived into the stream to find out where the deepest channel lay. Thus he was able to save a certain amount of unnecessary work, since the boom could be left over the shoals and sandbanks, clearing only the main channel which was well on the northern side of the river.

"I think that's done it, Petty Officer," he said at last. "I think there's a good clearance there."

"Ay, ay sir," said Hardbake cheerfully.

"I suggest we tow her out, eh? And then get the sails up once she's out of the creek and in fair water. I don't much fancy sailing her through that narrow opening."

"I'm with you, sir. Junks is rotten on the tiller—they yaws an' they falls away an' they behaves altogether conspicuous. I wouldn't sail a junk, not for choice, not nohow."

"Well, we'll rig up a tow, then. We can use both the small boat and the sampan. We won't leave anything behind to show which way we've gone."

They boarded the junk again and revealed their plans to the others. Colin hinted that there would be food forthcoming shortly, and Jack laughed.

89

"Once we're out of this and sailing downstream with the wind in our sails, then we'll eat."

Volunteers were called for to man the towing boats, and Jack himself took one of them. He left Hardbake at the junk's tiller and a couple of hands to rig the sail. The rest of the seamen all wanted to row the sampan or the small boat, but Jack told off Stacey for the job. The ropes were made fast, the mooring rope cast off, and the great adventure began.

Rowing with all his might, Jack wondered if the big junk would ever move. She was swinging lumpily in the slow waters of the creek, but showed no inclination to follow him. He could see Stacey in the sampan, straining at the big oar, the veins in his forehead standing out with the effort he was making, but apparently it was all without avail.

Then, suddenly, he seemed to be making headway. Suddenly the terrific pull was easier. He glanced back, and the big junk was moving slowly, majestically, through the water towards him. A cheer came from her decks. All was well!

Jack redoubled his efforts, and now the junk, emerging from the creek, met the waters of the river and swung like a shying horse towards the northern bank. Jack felt his boat being pulled off her course, and nearly cracked his giant oar with throwing his weight upon it. Out of the corner of his eye he could see Stacey's agonized face as he bent to his task, standing in the bows of the sampan, being dragged away towards the mudbank, towards the boom.

And then her nose came round and she curtsied towards them like a clumsy old charwoman at a ball. Jack nearly fell into the water as the strain was relaxed, but he held to his course and they drew her through the gap in the boom with very few feet to spare on either side.

"Come aboard, sir! I can git the sails up now," shouted Petty Officer Hardbake.

"Ay, ay," shouted Jack. "Come along Stacey. Our job's done." Then he cupped his hands and shouted to the junk. "Don't heave-to. Keep way on her. We'll cut the boats adrift and climb up the ropes."

"Climb up the ropes, sir, an' mebbe we'll be able to salvage the boats," advised the Petty Officer.

"As you say."

There was no time for more. The big sail was going up in short, jerky hoists, and the junk was bearing down on them. Jack manœuvred his boat to her starboard side and waited until she drew level. Then he swarmed up the tow-rope, which was being hauled taut by a party on the deck, and landed among them just as Stacey appeared on the opposite side.

"Excellent!" Jack said jubilantly. "How does she answer, Petty Officer?"

"Like a seasick cow, sir," was the mournful answer.

"Let me have the tiller a moment. Will you get those boats hauled up, if you can, and stowed away?"

"Ay, ay, sir."

91

Jack held the tiller, and had to admit that Hardbake's description had been fairly apt. She did answer to her helm, but only just. Still, the sail was filling with good, strong wind and the ripples were foaming out from her clumsy bows, and they were heading downstream away from the pirates. What more could anyone want?

"Ready for food, Captain?" asked Colin, appearing at Jack's elbow with a smile.

"You bet!" said Jack eagerly. "Have the wounded had anything?"

"Yes, I gave them some soup a little while ago. Pincher said he'd never get fat on that, but I don't think they ought to have too much, you know, at first."

"What about Curly?"

"He didn't want anything, but he took a little after some persuasion."

"And Carter?"

"He wouldn't have anything. I don't think he's fully conscious."

"I hope he's going to be all right."

"I hope so too, but I don't know."

"Well, take the lads below in shifts, will you? Petty Officer! Send the first watch below for a meal. Tell them to make it snappy, and when they come on deck again the second watch can go."

"Ay, ay sir."

"What about you?" asked Colin.

"All in good time. Or—you can bring me something up here if you like. When you've fed the lads. And yourself too."

"Ay, ay Captain," grinned Colin, and disappeared down to the galley again, followed by the seamen, who had suddenly discovered that they were starving.

Chapter 11

IN THE PIRATES' STRONGHOLD

IT was broad daylight when the first of the pirates opened his eyes and moved his aching head. After a little while he got up to get himself a drink, and presently kicked one of his comrades.

"Do you want to sleep all day as well as all night?" he growled.

"Leave me alone," grunted the other man.

"Get up!"

"No!"

The pirate drifted away and had another drink. Then another man joined him, yawning and grumbling. There were plenty of bad tempers on the plateau that morning.

When the Black Pirate himself awoke, things started to move. He shouted for someone to bring him a drink, and then cursed the man who brought it for being too long about it.

"Where are the others?" he asked, although he could see for himself that most of them were still sleeping.

"Asleep," was the morose reply.

"And the sentries?"

"Sentries? There are no sentries. They all joined in the fun last night and they're all sleeping now."

"Sleeping? They shall sleep with their ancestors before the day is out! Dogs! What if the foreign devils attack the camp while they are sleeping, and cut all our throats?"

"But we have the foreign devils," said the bandit reasonably. "How could they attack us when they are tied up?"

"We have not got all the foreign devils in the world tied up, fool that you are!" roared the Black Pirate. "There may be others already searching for their friends. Set sentries at once and wake the rest. I will not have this sleeping the day away. There is plenty to be done."

"True," said the bandit, brightening up as he remembered what they intended to do that day. He went off to awaken the rest.

The Black Pirate fumed and cursed, bit his nails as he glared at his men who were getting up in leisurely fashion. There was no discipline among them, and his orders were obeyed only if his men felt like doing so. If they were afraid of his mood they obeyed quickly enough, but once beyond the power of his angry eye they did much as they liked.

Now one man wandered off to the edge of the plateau, trailing a gun listlessly, and glanced perfunctorily over the countryside. The rest wandered about, quarrelling and cursing, one lighting the fire, another getting up the cooking pots, but all showing plainly the results of the heavy drinking of the previous night.

The Black Pirate sprang up from his rough couch and flung out among them, shouting and driving, giving orders and generally working off his evil temper. When he had them all moving more briskly he turned away, determined to visit the prisoners and wreak a little of his spleen on them.

A roar of rage startled the camp, and men came running up to him.

"Where are the prisoners? Who has dared to move the prisoners?" he shouted.

The men began to splutter denials, but the Pirate who was beside himself with fury, drew his knife, and rushed among them. Several received nasty cuts and slashes before they managed to get away, screaming that they knew nothing about the prisoners, had not moved them, and knew nothing—nothing at all.

Full of officious zeal now that his temper was really roused, the men hurriedly searched the caves and everywhere, but of course without result. Then the pieces of cut rope were found where Hardbake had hastily hidden them, and then the truth was out.

"They have escaped!"

Now the bandits blenched and drew back before the black fury of insane rage that gleamed in their leader's eyes. For a moment or two he stood mouthing incoherently, foam flecking his lips. Then with a scream he darted on the frightened sentry, stabbed him and tossed him over the cliff on to the rocks below.

"Who else was on guard last night? Who?"

There was no reply, and he grasped an evil-faced ruffian who could not elude him in time.

"Who was on guard last night? Answer, or I slit your throat."

"Li-Foo and Padabang," mumbled the man.

Li-Foo and Padabang!" The Pirate's eyes

moved round the circle balefully. "Li-Foo and Padabang. Bring them to me."

With a terrified shriek Li-Foo, a Chinese, threw down his gun and started to run down the mountainside, leaping from rock to rock in an ecstasy of terror. Padabang, the Malay, drew his kris and backed against the rocky side of the mountain that towered up one side of the plateau, and crouched in a defensive attitude.

"If he escapes, three men die," screamed the Black Pirate, and several shots rang out at once. The escaping Chinese leaped awkwardly into the air and fell in a crumpled heap.

"Bring him in. If he lives he shall taste what the prisoners would have had," said the Black Pirate, and turned his attention to the Malay. "Now shoot me this carrion."

And so it was that by the time the three sentries from the junk arrived, the Black Pirate was somewhat appeased by his revenge on his victims. Both were dead by this time, and he was organizing a hunt when the three arrived.

"Where are the prisoners?" they asked eagerly, coming round the rock and seeing only two corpses, evidently bandits, lying on the ground.

"Escaped," growled one of the men.

"Escaped?" shouted the sentry from the junk. "How? When? Where have they gone?"

"That's what we're going to find out. We're going to comb the whole country until we find them."

"Well, you need not take the area towards the

river," said the man confidently. "We've just come that way, and there was no one there."

"Tell that to the Master," said the other bandit, and the junk sentry swaggered over to where the Black Pirate was giving final instructions.

"What happened to my relief last night, Master?" he bawled familiarly as he approached.

The Pirate, whose temper was now recovered, grunted.

"What happened to all these dogs last night? They let the prisoners slip. No wonder they forgot your relief!"

"Too bad," said the sentry. "But we'll soon catch them again. We know which way they went."

"How do we know that?" demanded the Pirate.

"They did not go south-east to the river, or we should have seen them. They'd be fools if they went north over the mountain. They will have gone west, Master, depend on it. Easy country —just the thing for escaping prisoners. Only when they've got far enough away to feel safe will they realize there's nothing there for them and try to double back. Then we've got 'em."

"Yes Master, the country is bare to the west and north," said another man eagerly. "We have burned every village for a week's march to the west. They'll find no food and they'll have to come back. We can go out and pick them up at our leisure."

"We'll go out now and overtake them," said the Black Pirate. "First—who are the relief sentries for the junk?"

"Ming, Shosi and Padabang," said the man who had returned from that duty.

"Not Padabang, I think," purred the Black Pirate.

"Oh, is that Padabang there? I thought it looked a bit like him. Who then, Master?"

"Kem Rookh can go," said the Black Pirate. "And they had better go now. We will set off after the prisoners."

Of course it did not happen as briskly as that. The three men detailed to go to the junk wandered about, finding weapons, talking, arguing, eating a little, drinking a lot, and finally drifted off down the hillside at dusk. The main party who were to go after the prisoners set off shortly afterwards, preferring always to travel at night anyway.

It was quite dark when the three men arrived at the creek, and for a short while they wandered about aimlessly, trying to find the boat. When it did not come to light they curled up among the boulders to sleep until day. They were sure that only the darkness prevented them from finding it immediately.

They did not wake until the sun was high in the heavens, and then it was Shosi, the Jap, who took in the situation with one horror-stricken glance.

"The junk has gone!"

The others were alert at once, dashing down to the water's edge, searching among the reeds for their boat or the old sampan, and staring out across the creek as if they hoped that the junk would suddenly appear again if they stared hard enough.

"Is the boom still there?" asked Ming.

"We had better see," said Kem Rookh.

They set off to a point as near as they could get to the part of the river where the boom had been erected and could, of course, see that part of it at any rate was there.

"It is there!" said Shosi in an awed voice.

"Then how could the junk have gone?"

"Devils!"

"Foreign devils? The prisoners who escaped?"

"Possibly, but I think not," said Kem Rookh. "I think this is the work of witches. How else can a junk be made to rise in the air and fly over a boom?"

The other two agreed that this seemed to be the only explanation. With characteristic incompetence it did not occur to them to see if the whole boom was there intact. They could see that the part nearest to them was there, and that was enough. Now they squatted down on the beach and debated what they should do next.

"I do not intend to return," said Shosi after some talk. "The Master will be so angry at the loss of his junk that he will undoubtedly kill the first person who tells him about it."

"But where will you go?" asked Ming. "Where is there for us to go?"

"Not west, at any rate," said Kem Rookh.

"Certainly not west! And we know there is nothing for us either north or east. We will go south, and perhaps we shall find someone to help us on our journey. The Master has not yet travelled south, and there should be some fat cultivators who will be only too pleased to help three poor wanderers on their way. Oh yes, south is our road."

"We must first cross the river," observed Ming.

"True. Let us go eastward, first crossing the creek, until we find some fisherman who will lend us his sampan. After that it will be quite easy."

And so the three ruffians set off. They had to go inland for a little way until the creek was fordable, and then they made for the river bank. Sooner or later, they knew there would be a fisherman whose boat they could steal, and then, with the river between them and the Black Pirate, they would feel a great deal more comfortable.

Meanwhile the Pirate himself goaded his men on to the search. For some days they combed the countryside, but at last returned to their headquarters, dispirited and in an ugly temper. The Black Pirate had come to the conclusion that his prisoners had got clean away, and, having some experience of the dogged tenacity of Englishmen, felt that his fort was now in some danger. They had gone, but—quite rightly —he judged that they would return. He and his men had better go too.

Accordingly he had all their gear packed up into bundles which the men carried, coolie-fashion on their backs supported by straps round their foreheads, and they set off in a long straggling string down towards the river.

The Black Pirate himself headed the procession, carried in a litter by four of his men, and thus it was he who saw first of all that their vessel was not at her moorings. He cried to his bearers to hurry, and at last sprang out of the litter and ran to the creek, staring with unbelieving eyes at the empty water in front of him.

His men came up, shedding their bundles and chattering like magpies. With a fierce gesture he bade them be silent.

"Pambi—you can swim. See what has happened to the boom."

"It is still there, Master. I can see it," piped one of the bandits from the river bank.

"Fool—can you see right across? Pambi—swim out and make sure every inch of it is there."

It was just that extra little bit of carefulness that had raised the Black Pirate from the ranks of his slipshod, inefficient crew, and made him their feared leader. Now, to their admiration, he was proved right again. The middle section of the boom had gone.

The man stormed up and down the bank, cursing all foreign devils.

"They have killed Shosi, Ming and Kem Rookh!" he roared. "They have stolen my junk!" And he spent some minutes telling his admiring men exactly what he would do to the foreign devils when he caught them again.

After a while he calmed down, and made known his plans for the future.

"South," he said. "There should be plenty of villages and fat homesteads there that will sustain us until we can find another junk. I had planned to take that country next, and we will carry out that plan. First we must cross the river, and then we will march to the south."

Chapter 12

THE PARTING OF THE WAYS

"CAN you lend me the small boat, Jack?"

Jack Hawkins looked surprised at Colin's request.

"What on earth for?"

"Well, I want to go ashore somewhere about here. It's the nearest point to our village. I must get there and warn them before the pirates get to it."

"I'd forgotten," said Jack. "Yes, of course you must. Wait a minute—I want to think." He walked up and down the crowded deck for a moment or two, his head bent, deep in thought. He knew quite well what he wanted to do, and hoped it was his duty to do it. Presently he went below to find the Petty Officer.

"Mr. Hardbake—how many hands would you need to take this craft down to the sea?"

Petty Officer Hardbake looked up in surprise.

"'Ow many 'ands, sir? Was you think' o' goin' ashore, sir?"

"I was. I'm not sure about it yet. It depends very largely on whether you think you can manage without me. You see, Mr. Wedderburn wants to be put ashore pretty soon so that he can get to his father's village and warn the inhabitants. The Black Pirate is thinking of extending his tour in that direction. Of course, he'll possibly waste a few days looking for us, but it's practically inevitable that he'll go down that way sooner or later, and the village is defenceless."

"An' you want to take a few 'ands, sir, an' defend it?"

"That's about it."

"Well sir, as far as I'm concerned it's well enough. I can manage, sir."

"I knew you'd say that. Well, whom do you want to keep?"

"I don't think as I could manage with less than four, sir."

"I don't suppose you could."

"But, barrin' Martin, an' Robins an' Carter, I'll take the four worst wounded, sir. That leaves Stacey an' Binns an' Morrison for you, sir."

"Excellent!"

"An' you'll want this, sir." Petty Officer Hardbake slipped his revolver lanyard over his head and began to undo the webbing equipment.

"But—are you sure?" hesitated Jack. "I don't like to leave you weaponless."

"Oh! Didn't you know, sir? Some o' the lads found any number o' rifles—good ones, some of 'em—in a locker down below here. You take what you need, sir, an' leave us one or two, an' we shall do fine."

"I say, that's grand news!" exclaimed Jack.

"They're just here, sir."

Jack inspected the rifles, and found that some of them were, indeed, very good ones. Stolen, no doubt, but he could not go into that just then. Cases of ammunition were also found, and he at once got the Petty Officer to make up an amount for them to take with them.

That being settled, Jack found Stacey and

Binns, and informed them that he was planning another expedition against the Black Pirate. Binn's face was a study.

"Go on!" he ejaculated. Stacey spluttered with laughter.

"I'm game, sir," he said.

"I'm glad to hear it. Where's Morrison? I'd like him to come along too."

"'E's at the tiller, sir. But—'scuse me, sir—ain't you leavin' Mr. 'Ardbake a bit short-'anded, like?"

"He thinks he can manage. Mr. Wedderburn is coming with us, too."

"Oh, that's all right sir," said Binns with a confident grin. "That makes five of us. There's only fifty or so of them, ain't there?"

"About that," said Jack, and went off grinning.

Colin was on deck, watching the shore closely.

"Anywhere here," he said with a cheerful smile.

"Right you are. Like me to come with you?"

"I say!" Colin swung round, his eyes alight. "Do you mean it?"

"Of course I mean it. And I'm bringing three hands and some rifles with me."

"But that's grand! Don't the men mind?"

"Mind? They seem to think the odds are a bit unequal, as there are only fifty of them and five of us," said Jack.

Colin laughed.

"What splendid chaps they are!"

"Yes, they are. Now look here—can you draw a map?"

"Not a very good one, I'm afraid," said Colin, looking at his bandaged hands.

"It doesn't have to be a very good one. Just an indication of the direction and distance from the point where we go ashore, to your village. I'll give it to the Petty Officer and it'll help when Lieutenant Burgoyne—our captain—comes up river with the rest of the crew. That'll be the rendezvous. Can you do it?"

"Yes, I'll do it. Got a pencil and paper?"

Jack felt in his pockets and laughed.

"Not a sausage! Those scoundrels took everything. Wait—I'll ask Hardbake. He's the only man with any personal property left in this party."

Petty Officer Hardbake produced a pen and notebook, and Colin, with considerable difficulty, drew a map of the journey that he and Soo-Chu had made before they came in sight of the river. He marked in all the landmarks he could think of, and distances when he knew them, and it was quite a useful little guide when he had finished.

"Clear as a Admiralty chart, sir," said Petty Officer Hardbake with a smile. "Got the north in, sir?"

"North's up here, beyond the river."

"Ah, must put the north in sir! Now that's all ship-shape. Thank you, sir. I 'ope to be a-needin' that before many days is past."

Now the Petty Officer slackened sail and the junk lost way. The smaller boat was put down into the river and the five adventurers climbed aboard. Stores and ammunition and rifles followed them, and then the painter was cast off, the sail hoisted, and the junk gathered way again as they rowed to the bank.

"Best of luck!" shouted Jack as the big hulk swept past them, and even the wounded managed to lean up and wave.

"Same to you, sir!" shouted the crew of the junk, and a cheer rose, to be caught by the wind and carried away as the vessel continued on her way down to the sea.

"Well, you're the pilot now," said Jack as the boat nosed through the reeds to the bank. "Where do we go from here?"

"There's a path," said Colin, stepping ashore confidently and parting the reeds. "See? That's the way we came."

"Keep your eyes skinned, lads," said Jack, looking about him warily. "Although I don't suppose the blighters will have got as far as this already."

"Can't be too careful, sir," said Leading Seaman Stacey, remembering the ambush.

"You're right!"

Their march led them past the spot where Soo-Chu had been buried, and Colin spoke of him as they passed.

"I shall have to tell his mother," he said sadly. "I think it'll break her heart. She adored him."

"It's funny, but somehow I'd never thought of Chinese feeling the same about their children as English people do," said Jack.

Colin stared at him.

"Why ever not?"

"Well, they are different, aren't they?"

"Not at all. Different customs, perhaps, but inside people are much the same, I suppose, all over the world. I was brought up by Soo-Chu's mother—my own died when I was a baby—and really, she's just like any other mother. She's awfully gentle, of course. I mean, Chinese mothers don't smack their children as much as English people do, and Ngan Keng was a bit softer-hearted than most. But I expect some English mothers are on the soft side too, aren't they?"

Jack chuckled.

"I should say so! My young brother gets away with murder! Not that my mother would like to hear anyone say so. But I suppose, as you say, that people are pretty much alike all over the world. Except our friend the Black Pirate, of course. I don't think we've any like him at home."

Colin laughed.

"Well, that's just his luck, isn't it? I mean, plenty of people—even in England—are cruel or bad-tempered or dishonest. Only they can't be very bad because of the law. Here, where there isn't a policeman at every street corner, a man can be as bad as he likes. And so, on the other hand, if a man is good out here it means he is really good—good from the bottom of his heart—and not merely good because he's afraid to be anything else. That's where you find Christianity makes such a difference to people out here. They take it seriously and really make it a part of their lives. Of course they make mistakes, but everyone does that. But they don't go to church because it's the proper thing to do, as sometimes people do in civilized countries. If they go, it's because the whole thing is real to them."

"I suppose I shall make mistakes too," murmured Jack.

"I expect so," grinned Colin cheerfully. "You'd be a bit of a novelty if you didn't."

"It's nothing to be worried about, then?" asked Jack with some relief in his voice.

"Of course not! You will find, of course, that people who don't know anything about religion, and who won't bother to learn, take a very strict view about other people's faith. They think because a chap is trying to lead a decent life with God's help that he ought to be perfect all at once, and they say 'He's no better than anybody else! He's a hypocrite!' if a chap does go a bit wrong sometimes. But God tells us that if we do wrong as Christians, we are to confess it to Him and He promises to forgive and cleanse us. God knows all about us and it's being honest with him that counts—so Dad says, anyway, and I'd trust him to know what he's talking about."

Chapter 13

THE ATTACK ON THE VILLAGE

ON the third day after their landing, the little party reached the village. A few small boys saw them coming in the distance, and ran in to tell their parents. Mr. Wedderburn got his binoculars and focused them on the party, and recognized his son.

"I don't know who he's got with him," he said. "They appear to be armed. I'll go out and meet them."

Several people elected to go with him, and so Colin had quite a welcome on his return home. But his father noticed the bandages on his hands, and his eyes swept the group for the figure of Soo-Chu. His face grew very grave when he could not find him.

"I'll go ahead," said Colin when they were within shouting distance. "I'd like to get it over alone."

"Right you are," agreed Jack. "Give us a wave when you want us to come on."

Colin went ahead and Jack halted his men for a rest. They all understood why, and sympathized with the lad who had to break the news about the death of his companion.

"What happened?" asked Mr. Wedderburn swiftly as Colin reached him.

"Bandits, Dad."

"And Soo-Chu?"

"Dead!"

A horrified groan went up from the villagers. "Those are not—who are they?" asked Mr. Wedderburn, nodding towards Jack's party.

"That's a Naval party who rescued me. It's a long story, Dad, and I'd like to tell you all about it to-night. But we're tired and most of them are hurt. Will you put off explanations until later?"

"Of course." His father was about to pat him on the shoulder when the caked blood on the blouse caught his eye. "You're wounded?"

"Not seriously. I'll tell you all about it later on. Now I'd like to go back and see poor Ngan Keng, while you go and meet my friends. That's Jack Hawkins, the midshipman in charge of the party. He's a grand chap, Dad. A grand chap!"

Mr. Wedderburn went on, while Colin hurried back to the village to break the news to his foster-mother. It was a task that he dreaded, but he performed it faithfully, and by the time the rest returned Ngan Keng was calm again.

Meanwhile, seeing Mr. Wedderburn approach, Jack got his party going again although Colin had forgotten to give the signal of a wave, as agreed. The missionary held out his hand in greeting, and shook Jack's heartily.

"I hear you saved my son's life," he said. "I owe you a deep debt of gratitude for that."

"I think we all owe our lives to each other, sir," said Jack. "I owe him a great deal, as perhaps he'll tell you some day."

"He says he'll tell us all about it when he's

had a rest—when you've all had a rest and food and some medical attention. But I confess that I'm eager to hear. Bandits, he said. Can that really be so?"

"I'm afraid so," said Jack. "And the real reason why we're here is because we're bound to think they mean to attack down this way before long."

There was a rustle of consternation among the little crowd of people who had come out to meet them, most of whom knew a certain amount of English.

"I'm sorry to hear that," said Mr. Wedderburn, looking very grave. "We have absolutely no defences."

"We'll do our best for you. And it's fairly hopeful, because we've sent a message back to the ship and reinforcements will be coming. It's a question of holding out. Will you give me a free hand to choose the best defensive position?"

"Only too glad to," said Mr. Wedderburn. "And you can count on us all for every co-operation—you know that."

The tired little party marched into the village, and Mr. Wedderburn took them to his house, which was also the hospital—as far as the village ever needed a hospital. Here, at any rate, were the first-aid appliances, and now for the first time the various cuts and bruises received adequate attention.

While this was being done, the Chinese women hurried to prepare food, and foremost among them was brave Ngan Keng. The hungry men ate as they had not eaten for more than a week, and then threw themselves down, just as they were, to sleep.

"If you'll allow me sir, I'd like to walk round and see about that defensive position now," said Jack.

"What about the church?" asked Colin, whose shoulder was at last being bathed and inspected. He winced slightly as the blood-caked pad came off.

"That's fine," said his father briskly. "It's healing splendidly. Just wants a clean piece of lint and a bandage and you'll be perfectly all right. I'm not so pleased about the hands, though. How on earth did you get them into that condition?"

"That's all part of the story," said Colin. "But what about my suggestion, Jack? The church is the stoutest building in the place—what about putting all the women and children in there?"

"I don't advise it," said Mr. Wedderburn. "From what I know of these pirates, I don't advise it. I know we haven't had any trouble in these parts for a good many years, but I do remember that one of their habits was to throw burning darts into the thatch of any building, thus turning it into a death-trap."

"Yes, I don't think the church would be any use as a fort," said Jack. "It's too much hemmed in, for one thing. They could get too near. No. Let me go and wander round, and you tell your father our story, Colin. It'll interest him!"

So while Colin and his father sat and talked in

the cool of the evening and the weary seamen slept, Jack walked round the village and wished, in his heart of hearts, that he had Petty Officer Hardbake there to advise him. However—he was not there! Jack squared his shoulders and made up his mind to do the best he could without him. When, an hour later, he returned to the missionary's house, he had his plan.

"Oh, there you are Jack," cried Colin as the shadowy form loomed up through the twilight. "What about it?"

"I think we must fortify that hill. I don't think we can possibly hope to hold the village, but the hill doesn't look too hopeless. I'd like all the able-bodied men in the place to get to work digging earthworks as soon as possible, sir. Can that be done?"

"Of course," said Mr. Wedderburn. "I think they all know by now what we are faced with and they'll be only too pleased to do whatever they can to help."

"That's splendid! And are there any out-lying farms that ought to be brought in? Fisher-men or anything?"

"I've thought of that. All the small boys have gone out to bring them in. I think they should all get here some time during the night."

"That's excellent! Then, if the women could bring all the bedding and food stores and all that sort of thing up to the top of the hill and rig up shelters for the children that would help. I think, sir, it would be best if we could all get up there to-night. I don't know how soon they'll be coming this way, but I'd rather not be caught napping a second time."

Mr. Wedderburn agreed to this and soon the night was full of activity. Dozens of lanterns burned, hanging from trees or standing on the ground, little glowing spots of light all round the hill, where the men were digging under Jack's instructions, and to and fro from the houses, which the women and children were emptying of their treasures, carrying them up the hill into the big circle that was being excavated for them.

Under the willing work of the Chinese, aided now by the seamen, the earthworks rose as if by magic. A great wall of earth right round the top of the hill gave protection on every side, and down behind it the defenders could move about in perfect safety. Into this fort all the bedding was moved, all the food, all the medical supplies. Mr. Wedderburn then brought his cherished communion vessels from the little church, and some of the other furnishings. At last the village stood empty, and Mr. Wedderburn told the women and children to get some sleep.

The digging went on. In Jack's opinion the wall could not be too thick! When he had got the depth inside to his requirements he started the diggers on a deep ditch outside, to make attack more difficult. A narrow opening was left in the wall and filled with brushwood. If there were time Jack hoped to get a stout gate made, but in the meantime the brushwood was the best he could think of.

Next day passed quietly. Leading Seaman

Stacey wanted to sink a well, but Mr. Wedderburn did not think this was practicable. They filled everything they could think of with water, but it was obvious that, in the event of a siege, this was going to be their difficulty. There were the animals to be thought of—the hens and the cows and the pigs. However, it was devoutly hoped that the *Panther's* men would relieve them before the situation became acute.

The day passed quietly. The sentries watched keenly, aware that the pirates might be along any time now. The women and children stayed in the fort, but the men went outside, bringing in more water and some vegetables, taking care, however, not to be surprised by any creeping bandit.

They settled down to the second night inside the earthworks. The moon was obscured behind racing clouds, and a light wind was blowing. There was no sound, and the sentries strained their eyes to see into the darkness. The lanterns were out, for Jack considered that it would be better not to disclose their position until it was necessary. All was dark and all was quiet.

Suddenly a little streak of flame ran up the thatch of one of the cottages on the outskirts of the village. It flickered for a minute or two, and then the whole thatch was ablaze. Another, and then another caught fire. The pirates had come.

At the first flicker, the sentry had roused Jack, and Mr. Wedderburn had gone with him to the wall and watched the burning. In silence the rest of the men were roused and went to their posts. Mr. Wedderburn had several guns, and with them he armed some of the Chinese, with orders on no account to shoot unless a pirate was practically at the end of the barrel. Colin, of course, had one of the guns, and took his place with the rest at the defensive positions.

Puzzled by the silence of the place, the pirates began to leave their cover and to come into the village, openly setting fire to the houses, and running from one to another shouting with rage as they found them all empty. Then Jack gave the word to fire.

"Pick your man. Don't waste a single bullet."

The first volley sent half a dozen of the pirates to the ground, and the rest raced for cover. There was no more shooting for a little while, but the quiet night was torn by the roaring of the flames and the crackling of the blazing cottages. Jack went over to the far side of the fort.

"Keep your eyes skinned this side," he said, blinking as he tried to accustom his eyes to the darkness again, after the lurid glare of the fire. "It won't take 'em long to discover where we are, and then they'll creep up like cats. Don't let them find you asleep."

"No sir," said Binns, "They won't do that, sir."

It was not long before the expected attack came. With a terrifying shriek, the pirates attacked on the side farthest from the village, as Jack had expected. After a brisk battle during which more than one pirate came to his end, they retired.

"End of Round One!" laughed Jack. "I wonder what they'll think up for Round Two?"

Chapter 14

PANTHER TAKES ACTION

CHIEF Petty Officer Birkett stood on the bridge of H.M.S. *Panther* and fixed his binoculars on an object pointed out to him by the look-out.

"It is!" he said with satisfaction. "It's the junk, all right. Anson! My compliments to Mr. Burgoyne, an' the junk's bin sighted."

Burgoyne was on the bridge in a moment, staring through his telescope at the vessel sailing down the river towards the sea.

"Action stations!" he snapped. Then he turned to the other man. "But I wish I knew what had happened to our landing party. How on earth did they come to let them get away?"

The deck was a scene of orderly activity. Gun crews were getting their weapons ready and boarding parties were strapping on cutlasses and small arms. Then the look-out shouted again.

"Carrying some sort of flag, sir."

"Skull and crossbones, I suppose," said Burgoyne, turning his glass upon it. "What do you make of it, Chief?"

There was such a long silence after his question, that he turned with a look of inquiry.

"Can't you make it out?"

"Well sir, it looks—well, it looks like an Ensign, sir!"

"What?" Lieutenant Burgoyne applied himself again to his telescope. "It is, too! Well I'm hanged! What cheek!"

"What will you do sir?"

"Do? I'm not going to let him get away with that. If he thinks that sailing under false colours is going to get him off the just punishment he's going to get, well, he's mistaken."

"He's heaving to, sir," said the Chief Petty Officer after a moment or two.

"Now what's his game?" pondered Burgoyne.

"Lowering a boat, sir."

"Make a signal—'Who are you?'" directed Burgoyne and this was done.

No answering string of bunting was shown, but instead the flicker of an electric torch gave the reply, which was read in an undertone by every man on deck.

"H.M.S. *Panther* boarding party, under the command of Petty Officer Hardbake."

"Well, I'm hanged!" ejaculated Lieutenant Burgoyne. "But what's happened to poor Hawkins, I wonder? Ah well—here comes their boat. We shall soon know now."

Petty Officer Hardbake was soon on board, telling his story. Colin's map was compared with a large-scale map of the district in Burgoyne's cabin, and immediate action decided upon. The wounded were brought into the gunboat's tiny sick bay—poor Carter had died on the way down river, but the others were making good progress—and Lieutenant Burgoyne, when he was satisfied that he had all the details, sent Petty Officer Hardbake to his bunk with orders not to stir until sent for.

"I shan't be sorry, sir," said Hardbake with a

faint grin. "But call me if there's anythink going, won't you, sir?"

"Yes, you old fire-eater, I will. But meanwhile get some sleep. Even you can't go on for ever without a rest."

"No sir. Thank you sir." Hardbake saluted and went below.

Preparations now went forward with speed. The gunboat nosed her way up the river, and Burgoyne chose the men he intended to take with him when he went to the defence of the village. He had been much relieved to find that Jack Hawkins had not been killed and was even now probably fighting the Black Pirate, but he quite realized the necessity for haste. The odds were desperate—fifty against five—and he sent his men to rest with the warning that it would be a matter of forced marches once they left the ship until they made contact with the bandits.

"Hello Hardbake, what are you doing here?" inquired Lieutenant Burgoyne as the Petty Officer appeared at his elbow on the bridge.

"I think as we're gettin' close to the disembarkation spot, sir."

"I see. You didn't think you were coming with us by any chance?"

"What, me sir? Well sir, 'avin' bin in close contact, as you might say, with the Pirate, I thought as naturally you'd want me along."

"Oh, you did, did you? Well, Chief Petty Officer Birkett thinks it's his turn."

"Birkett sir?" Hardbake laughed pityingly. "Beg pardon sir, but you're jokin', o' course.

Birkett, he's new to these waters. He don't speak the lingo, sir. An' he's young, sir. I know 'e's a Chief, sir, an' good luck to 'im—funny things 'appen in the Navy these days!—but 'e don't know these parts, sir. Beggin' your pardon, sir, but he's just the man to leave in charge o' the ship when we goes ashore. 'E can't do no 'arm there, sir."

"Hardbake, you're greedy," said Burgoyne with a chuckle. "I'm afraid it is Birkett's turn. Now what's the least number you'll want left behind with you?"

"I'll keep the wounded and a couple o' 'ands, sir," said Hardbake philosophically.

"Is that enough?"

"Plenty, sir. I've got the guns. If there's any trouble I reckon I can 'andle it."

Burgoyne was sure of his ability to do so, and gave instructions that as soon as his party were ashore Hardbake was to take the gunboat down river again. The junk was now moored well off shore, and *Panther* was to take up her original station until sent for. A small portable transmitting set went with the landing party and would be used to send a message when they wanted to be taken off again.

Hardbake put them ashore and then took the gunboat down to the sea again. The engine-room crew was of course, still with him, and the other non-combatant members—the cooks and sick-berth attendants—also. But most of the able-bodied fighting men were with Lieutenant Burgoyne.

Burgoyne found the path quite easily and led his men down it at a spanking march. The march was not quite so spanking next day, for he had kept them at it all night, with brief rests for refreshment occasionally. However, no one grumbled, and on they went until their tired footsteps got quite miraculously brisk at the sound of distant firing.

"This is where we start going carefully," said Burgoyne. "We don't want to give ourselves away. Make for that hill. We might be able to see something from there."

They climbed the hill, and there saw, far to the south, another hill with little puffs of smoke around it, and a big pall of smoke to one side of it.

"That's a burning village," exclaimed Burgoyne, with his binoculars on it. "And there's a battle royal going on round that hill. There's something—a flag—yes!—an Ensign! On we go, lads. That's where they are!"

The defenders of the little fort had no idea that help was so near. Indeed, it seemed as though help could not come soon enough to be of any use to them now. They were reeling with weariness, faint with hunger and light-headed with thirst. The frightened babies were crying continuously, adding a horrible background to the noise of the firing and the terrifying shrieks of the pirates. So far none of the children had been hurt, and by Jack's orders they, at least, had not suffered the lack of food and water, but stocks were running low, and what would happen when they ran out no one liked to think.

The Ensign had been made by the women, sitting crouching with their little ones under the shelter of the big earth wall. What it was made of, nobody asked; one of the sheets from Mr. Wedderburn's bed, perhaps—the bed that was now burned together with his house and all his treasures. Stacey had helped with advice during the occasional lulls, and it was Stacey who had managed somehow to rig it up, and who replaced it every time the pirates shot it down.

Jack was glad that he was fighting under the old Ensign. His head was ringing with weariness and his face was covered with blood from a glancing shot that had seared his cheek. He was sure now that this was his last fight, and he liked to think that if he fell the Ensign would be there to cover him. Though who would be left alive to do so, if that happened, he did not stop to think. Probably nobody.

"They're going to make another rush, sir," called Binns hoarsely.

"Coming," said Jack, and dragged himself to his feet. He loaded his revolver again, and went over to the parapet.

"Here they come!"

A burst of fire crackled in the distance, but it did not come from the pirates, who stopped their headlong forward rush, wavered uncertainly, and seemed to melt into the undergrowth.

"That's a Lewis! That's a Lewis!" shouted Jack as the distant chatter of a machine gun came to his ears. "Thank God! The Navy is here!"

Chapter 15

THE END OF A MENACE

IT was a short, sharp engagement, but although the advantage in numbers still rested with the pirates the advantages in weapons did not. They had suffered severe losses in their attacks on the fort, too, and this last enemy was too much for them. They ran headlong in all directions, but before long all were rounded up and brought back for justice.

"What do you intend to do with them?" asked Mr. Wedderburn, looking at the gang of unsavoury rascals. "Hang them?"

"No, I shall just take them back to the base and hand them over to the authorities," said Lieutenant Burgoyne. "I'm glad to say it isn't my job to be judge and executioner as well as policeman!"

"What will you do now?" Jack asked Colin. "The village is a total wreck! What on earth will the people do?"

"Rebuild," said Colin quietly. "It won't be so bad, you know. This is a wonderfully fertile country. All this stuff will soon grow again, and most of the cows and hens were saved."

"What are they doing?" asked Jack, for all the villagers seemed to be congregating together in one spot.

"I think they've asked Dad to take a Service of Thanksgiving," said Colin. "Yes—there he goes."

"Well, can't we join in?"

"I was hoping you'd want to."

"Of course. I'll just get the lads together—" Jack leaped to his feet and went off to find Lieutenant Burgoyne, who was chatting to the Chief Petty Officer.

"Sir," said Jack saluting smartly, "Mr. Wedderburn is just going to hold a Thanksgiving Service. Er—may I find out if any of the hands would like to attend?"

"Certainly," said Burgoyne, looking surprised. "But—looking at the charred mess that they've made of his village—I don't know what they've got to be thankful for!"

"They're alive, sir," said Jack grimly. "A few hours ago none of us thought we should be much longer!" He saluted, and went off to find the men.

"That lad's steadied up a bit," said Lieutenant Burgoyne, staring after him. "I should never have thought that services of any sort, thanksgiving or not, would have been much in his line. I think I'll go along too, Chief. Coming?"

"Ay, ay sir," said Chief Petty Officer Birkett, who took the line that what his commanding officer did was good enough for him. And so, when Mr. Wedderburn came out to take the simple service, he found not only his own people, but a fine display of the Royal Navy waiting for him. For that, as for their deliverance, the missionary gave thanks.

Jack and Colin had a last talk together the following day, before the march back to the ship began. Colin broached a subject that he thought would be important to his friend, and he was right.

"I spoke to Dad about what you said that night when we were tied up in the pirates' stronghold, before old Hardbake came and rescued us."

"What did he say?" asked Jack, going rather red.

"Well, he was glad, of course. But what I asked him about mostly was that question of yours—whether you would have to give up the Navy and become a missionary if you took—er—things seriously."

"What did he say to that?" asked Jack anxiously.

"He said the same as I did—were you willing to do so?"

"I'm willing, of course," said Jack steadily. "If that's what my Captain orders, well I'll obey."

"But you're not keen?"

Jack was silent.

"Come on, Jack! Speak up! Honestly, now?"

"Honestly—not keen," said Jack slowly.

"You don't feel a call to the job?"

"I—I'm afraid not. Do you?"

"Me? I think it's the most glorious work in the world, and I wouldn't do anything else—wait a minute, I was going to put my foot in it there. I wouldn't do anything else unless I was quite convinced that it was my Heavenly Father's will that I should."

"Well, there must be something wrong with me, then," said Jack. "Because that's how I feel about the Navy."

"You silly old ass! No, there's nothing wrong with you, Jack. Don't you see that you can serve God just as faithfully in the Navy as any-where else? He doesn't want everyone to throw up their jobs and rush to become missionaries. He wants you to be a good Christian just where you are. If He does want you to leave the Navy, though, it'll be made quite clear to you. You'll suddenly start to feel about the missionary life as I do—that it's the only life in the world. If that happens your course is clear, but until it does, you stay where you are."

"Whew!" Jack's face brightened and he squared his shoulders. 'You've taken a load off my mind!"

"That sounds good," said Mr. Wedderburn, coming up to join them. "What's he done?"

"Told me I didn't have to be a missionary," grinned Jack.

Mr. Wedderburn chuckled.

"You can be an unofficial missionary without a dog-collar," he suggested. Jack looked puzzled, and he continued: "Every man who loves Jesus and who tries to please Him in all he says and does is a missionary really. Here's a text you may find helpful: 'Whatsoever thy hand findeth to do, do it with all thy might, as unto the Lord'. It may not be as spectacular as some things, but it's the most useful sort of life there is. Doing whatever God sends for you to do, well and cheerfully, trusting in the Spirit of Christ to give you the necessary strength and power, whatever the job may be. If you do that, then you're a missionary all right."

"Sometimes it's spectacular too," said Colin. "Like fighting pirates."

"And sometimes it isn't!" grinned Jack. He held out his hand. "I don't know how I can ever thank you for—well—you understand."

"And how are we to thank you for saving our lives?" smiled Mr. Wedderburn.

"Me?" Jack laughed. "It was a grand scrap! I say—they're forming up to march off! I shall have to hurry. I'd like to come and look you up again some time, if I may. Good-bye—I'll remember what you said, sir. Good-bye, Colin. If ever you get into an argument with a pirate again, just send for me! Good-bye!" He ran off and joined the Naval party, now ready to escort their prisoners back to the ship and thence to the base. Burgoyne smiled and returned his salute, and then, his own farewells being said, gave the order to march.

Colin and his father stood on the wall of the fort, surrounded by the villagers, and watched them until they were merely a moving thread in the distance. The sun glinted from time to time on their weapons. Then at last they were gone.

"Grand fellows!" said Mr. Wedderburn. "Now —whatsoever thy hand findeth to do—there's plenty to do here! Let's get busy."